About the Author

I am Leonie and I have been writing *The Step Love* ever since I was sixteen, which is two years ago, and I enjoyed every minute and day. I also love creating characters and stories to become books. I am a new author and I hope you all love my first book as much as I did writing it.

The Step Love

The Step Love

Leonie Rhule

Olympia Publishers
London

www.olympiapublishers.com
OLYMPIA PAPERBACK EDITION

A CIP catalogue record for this title is
available from the British Library.

ISBN: 978-1-78830-031-5

First Published in 2018

Olympia Publishers
60 Cannon Street
London
EC4N 6NP

Printed in Great Britain

Dedication

To my mum and dad, who showed me you can be anything if God is by your side.

Acknowledgments

I thank everyone at the Olympia team for helping me do corrections for this book while it was a hard start. I also thank my lovely family and cousins who comforted me to bring Tommy to life no matter what the problem was and who supported me through the process. Now Tommy is out there for you guys to read. I thank most of my book social media friends, who can't wait to read Tommy and also helped me to bring his life and troubles to the world to hear. I thank my mum and dad for helping me write this book or it wouldn't even be in your hands.

Chapter One

I'm Tommy Dawson. My mother died when I was eight years old due to a car accident. Since the accident, I lived with my dad and my little brother Daniel, who was seven years old, in a house two minutes away from California beach. I hated our house because it was small and dusty.

One day whilst in my cramped house, I was playing with Daniel in the corner, as there was no space. Dad came to us saying, "Boys, I got a new job. It's an office job but it's far away from home, so we might be moving this Monday."

Then I said, "Are we going to see Harriet, Dad?"

She was the new girl Dad has been dating since my mom died, but she wasn't nice to me. I looked down at Daniel, nodded to see if he okay with the idea, and Daniel gave me a sad look, which made my nerves shake.

***

Monday arrived really quickly, and Dad came to my room to wake me up. I groaned and turned to my side.

Dad said, "Tommy, wake up. Today is our move to the new house."

I mumbled and whined. "Dad, just a few minutes. I'm still tired and I don't want to wake up now."

But Dad wasn't convinced, so he pulled the covers and the sheets. I was shivering – I wasn't wearing a t-shirt. I was just in my boxers and racing cars socks.

I looked at the sun with one eye open, and then I got up as I was told to, so I could freshen up in the bathroom by seven a.m.

Every morning, I brushed my teeth and showered, and then I went to my room and I put on some clothes. When I got dressed up I went downstairs, while Daniel was already prepared. I got in the car and Dad parked at the new house.

I got out, looking at the building. I froze without saying a word when I heard, "Oh, it's Tommy. How lovely to see you!"

Then my stepmother Harriet appeared to see us. Dad and Harriet were now inside, and with Daniel holding my hand, I walked in slowly with him.

The house was old, haunted and dusty, with spider webs everywhere.

Chapter Two

From the outside, the sun appeared to beam in through the window, and the light shone. But it was a bit dark through the glass, and when Daniel and I got inside we couldn't see Dad because of the fog and dust.

I shouted, "Dad! Can you see us?"

Then I coughed, because the dust went through my throat every time I spoke. We coughed and coughed for a while, until the dust cleared and we found Dad in the living room at last.

Harriet wasn't as scary as I thought she would be, but she was strict at times, like when a bit of pee landed on the floor instead of the toilet – she'd go mad with me.

But ever since my mom passed away, I had a hard time controlling my bladder, and Dad wasn't very good at waking me up every night to make me use the bathroom – most times he was drunk and fell asleep.

Until one night, when Daniel and I went to sleep, I got up and heard Harriet and Dad talking about me. Harriet said that I was a good boy and that she should be helping me and Daniel more.

I almost slipped on the stairs as I struggled to take my feet away so I wouldn't fall. My heart beat harder as I watched my feet slip down.

"Ahh!" I went, as Daniel got up.

He said, "Tommy, where are you?"

"Daniel, I'm down here."

Daniel leaned over, reached for my hand and pulled me up. Dad looked up – no one was there. By then Daniel and I had gone to bed.

I lay on my bed looking up at the ceiling, wondering when tomorrow would be here. I eventually fell asleep and then it was morning.

Chapter Three

Daniel came in. He said, "Tommy, wake up!"

I groaned as the sun went into my eyes, and I said, "I'm awake, Daniel," as I rubbed my eyes. I swung my legs over the bed and got up. I went to the bathroom, took the toothbrush and started brushing my teeth, while Daniel stayed by my side. As I finished, I went downstairs with him to see what was going on. Flashbacks went into my mind every time I remembered how my dad behaved towards me when I was little. How scary Harriet was when I met her the first day.

I went outside to play with Daniel. It was almost my thirteenth birthday, and I was excited for it. Then I went back inside the house with Daniel and sat down in the living room, while Dad was asleep and Harriet was making our dinner.

Daniel went into the computer room while I watched TV. Daniel looked around as a book fell and hit his head. Then he got up and wondered what it was. The moment he opened it, he realised it wasn't an original book.

The book talked about how kids struggled away from their parents, and how they don't like living with their new parents.

"Tom!" Daniel shouted.

"Yes?" I replied.

I don't like being called Tom because my mom used to call me that, and every time I hear "Tom" I think of her.

Chapter Four

I said, "What is it Daniel?" I got up, walked over to the computer room and looked around. I gasped, looking at him in shock. "Did you make all this mess, Daniel?"

"No, I didn't!" Daniel responded, looking at the floor and not meeting my eyes. "Where did this book come from?"

I lied and said, "It's nothing to do with you."

As I grabbed it out of his hand and put it back on the shelf. Daniel looked at me, puzzled. I bent down as Daniel watched me cleaning the mess, and then he joined in with me.

It was getting dark in Los Angeles, and our new house wasn't so close to the beach. By the time Daniel and I were done cleaning the room, it was six p.m. and we went to have our dinner.

After eating, I went upstairs to have a shower. I then dried myself, got into my pyjamas, went to my room and climbed into bed.

I woke up and it was another weekday. Today was my first day at Northern Hills Middle School.

I thought about how everything had changed: new school, new friends, and new teachers. Of course, I might have bullies, but every school has them.

Chapter Five

I went to the bathroom and took a shower. Then I dried off and went to my room to get dressed for my first day.

Daniel was downstairs, already dressed, and watching TV before breakfast. I ran downstairs and said, "Good morning, Harriet," as I tried to sound cheerful.

She looked at me with her lime green eyes while getting our bowls ready, and she said, "Morning, Tom. Today is your first day at Northern Hills Middle School."

I sat down at the table with Daniel. "Yes, it is, Harriet." I played with my fingers, looking down. I was a bit nervous since it was my first day. I wondered what the teachers and my new friends would think of me.

When I was done having breakfast, I got my bag, got on my bike and started riding to school. Once I got to the gate, I parked my bike and went in.

The school smelt like a hospital – it was clean and had a strong medical scent, and the corridor was quiet and empty. I walked to find room A12, which was my form room for the school year.

Chapter Six

I went in and sat down on the floor, waiting for my new teacher to introduce us. She came and unlocked the door, and I went in with my new classmates.

Miss Ranford said, "Hello, class. I am Heather Ranford, your A12 teacher for the year." Then she wrote it on the whiteboard with a red marker pen which shone on the board.

I stayed quiet, looking for a place to sit, and then she called out, "Class, today we have a new student with us." She told me to come over.

I slowly walked over to the front and looked down, while I mumbled, not wanting to speak loudly, "I'm Tommy Dawson..."

Miss Ranford said, "Tommy, sweetie, speak a bit louder so the class can hear you."

I repeated myself in a slightly louder voice. "I am Tommy Dawson, and I just moved here."

I looked down, and then I walked to my seat and sat down. When I looked up at the board, I heard kids three rows down from me laughing as I looked at my "All About Me" worksheet.

I wondered what they were laughing about, but I didn't pay any notice, and I finished the worksheet.

Chapter Seven

I have dirty light brown hair. My eyes were brown, but got darker. Sometimes my skin is a bit tanned, and I have a few freckles near my nose and eyes. I speak with a Scottish sort of accent, even though I am American.

I finished my worksheet and got up. Then I went to the boys' toilets. I didn't know how long I stayed there for, but by the time I got out the break was over. It seemed weird staying in the toilets for break, but I didn't like the new students in my class.

Then I went back to class and sat down at my desk, listening to Miss Ranford for our last lesson. Then the class was over and I went to pick up Daniel from school, and then I went home.

I went inside the house with Daniel and took off my tie, which was pinching me. I didn't like wearing a tie with my school uniform – in fact, I hated it.

I went to the fridge before taking off the rest of my school uniform, and looked to see if I could have a snack bar. Daniel went to his room, and I sat down in the living room watching TV.

Harriet came over and asked, "Tom, how was your first day at school?"

I responded, "It was fine, Harriet. I enjoyed it."

I concentrated on watching the TV, and then I fell asleep. I didn't know how long I slept for, but I was really tired, and by the time I woke up it was time for dinner.

Daniel was sitting next to me. "Hey, Tom," he said, looking into my eyes and smiling a little.

"Hey, Danny," I responded, while groaning with sleep in my eyes and struggling to keep one eye open to look up at him.

I got up, went to the kitchen and got ready for dinner with Daniel. He followed me, and then we sat down and ate. After we had dinner, Daniel and I decided to go to the park with Dad and my stepmother for the evening.

Chapter Eight

I put on my coat and hat. Then Dad opened the door and we all walked down to Great Dale Grant Park, which wasn't far from our house. Dad and Harriet sat down on the bench. Daniel and I played tag, and then I bumped into a girl behind me.

"Ouch!" the girl said. "Look where you're going." She brushed the dirt off her dress.

"I'm sorry, I didn't see you there," I said, looking a bit embarrassed.

She said, "My name is Sarah," while looking at the ground, and played with her fingers.

I said, "My name is Tommy," while looking down, feeling shy.

"Nice to meet you, Tommy," Sarah said cheerfully, looking at her watch. I could hear it ticking.

She was tall with long, brunette hair and a few freckles under her eyes, and she was skinny, her figure showing through the dress she wore.

Chapter Nine

Sarah explained to me that she had been in the neighbourhood for a while and asked me if I needed any help. She was willing to support me.

I said, "Oh, thank you, Sarah."

Then I saw Daniel running back to me, his little Converse covered in mud. He giggled, saying he had fun, and as he looked into Sarah's eyes he said, "Hello." He was even shyer than I was, and he looked at me instead.

Sarah bent down to Daniel's height and smiled at him. "Hello, sweetie."

I took Daniel by the hand and said, "We must be going home now – it's going to rain."

We both said bye to Sarah, and then we started walking to where Dad and Harriet were sitting, getting ready to go back to the house.

Dad said to me, "You've started making friends here, kiddo – that's good for you."

I said, "I am getting used to everyone and things here."

Dad smiled at me, and I smiled back at him.

We got to the door and Dad opened it. We went in and took our coats off. I was glad we were home before it started raining.

I went to the computer room and sat down to do some of my homework.

The power went out, and I fell trying to find the light. I felt someone grab me tight, and I sensed Harriet pulling me hard.

"Dad! Tell her to let me go!" I screamed at the top of my lungs, and my heart started to beat faster as I struggled to get free.

Chapter Ten

Harriet's hands were so stiff and tight that I fainted to the floor, and then I woke up and looked around the room.

Dad came over to me and said, "Are you all right, Tom?"

I said, "Yes, I am fine, Dad."

I was confused, and then I thought for a while. It was just a dream – nothing happened. I kept telling myself this to prevent panic attacks.

I went to my room to have a lie down. Daniel came and sat on the floor, playing with his toy car. I looked at the ceiling while Daniel had fun playing. I stretched and sat up to look at what Daniel was doing.

Daniel smiled and continued playing around, and then I got up, went to the bathroom and looked in the mirror.

I missed my mother. It didn't feel the same being with Harriet, and I still experienced echoing thoughts about my stepmother that made my ears ring.

I screamed so loud that Daniel ran suddenly to check on me. I told him I was fine and that I'd be in the room to play with him soon.

I went back to my room, sat down and picked up my laptop. I looked around online, and then I typed in "Boys' Games for Pre-teens".

I picked snake and ladders and started playing with this boy from Britain. He was a bit younger than I expected, because he was eleven and I would be thirteen the next day.

But we talked about stuff we liked on the chat until I told him I was going downstairs, and then I shut my laptop and went down with Daniel.

Harriet and Dad were sitting down watching TV with a cup of hot chocolate.

Dad smiled and said, "Tomorrow is your birthday, Tom, so what do you want to do?"

I said, "Dad, I want to go and watch the new *Action Man 3*."

Dad sighed and said, "Okay, Tom, we will go."

"Okay, Dad!"

I jumped around, feeling super happy. We sat around and watched TV until it got dark.

Chapter Eleven

I saw Daniel fall asleep on the couch, blowing bubbles like a baby train letting out steam, and I smiled, stroking his hair softly. I looked at the TV, and then I yawned, feeling sleepy.

I said to Harriet, "Daniel and I are going to bed."

Harriet replied, "Okay, Tommy. Goodnight."

I slowly picked up Daniel, and his arms dangled down my back. I started walking up the stairs.

I felt achy and numb. I continued walking, and by the time I got to the top I was breathing heavily, but I didn't want to let Daniel fall, so I held him tightly. I walked slowly to the room, trying not to fall since my feet were so weak and floppy, as I lightly put Daniel into his bed. Then I went to my room, got into bed, and fell asleep.

***

When I woke up, it was morning. It was my birthday, and I was officially thirteen. I got out of bed, went to the bathroom and brushed my teeth. I went to my room, changed into my school uniform, put on my shoes and went downstairs.

Downstairs was quiet as usual. Dad was on the sofa watching the news with Daniel, who was dressed in his school uniform.

Harriet was making breakfast. She came over and said, "Happy birthday, Tom."

I smiled as I was given my present from Harriet, Dad and Daniel. It was a small watch which had my name on it, and the hands changed colour.

I thanked Harriet, Dad, and Daniel, and then I opened the door.

Chapter Twelve

I started walking to the bus stop. The weather was breezy and cold, and my hands were numb from the blizzard feeling.

I managed to reach the bus stop, and then I put my headphones in my ears and started listening to music, watching my feet tap to the beat on the ground. I prayed the bus would come quickly because it was too cold to be waiting.

Eventually the bus came, and I got on and went to find myself a seat.

I noticed someone say, "Tommy," in a soft, gentle voice. I turned to look beside me, and I realised it was Sarah.

"Hi, Sarah," I responded, and then I took out one of my earbuds to hear her voice probably. Sarah and I spoke for a while, until the bus stopped at school and we both went our separate ways.

After school, I decided to stop by my mother's grave and tell her how much I missed her. I rang Harriet and lied that I was going to see one of my friends, so I'd come home a bit late.

I went to Great Grand Enchanted Park where my mother was buried. Then I saw my mom's grave: "Susan Ann Dawson".

I got down on my knees, hugged the stone and cried, saying in my sobs, "Mom, I miss you. Why did you have to leave me? The world doesn't feel the same without you now!"

I took off my school uniform tie and wrapped it around my mom's gravestone. I kissed the stone, and then I got up and ran before someone saw me.

By the time I got out of the park it was dark already. I started walking back to the house. It was raining so my uniform was wet. My feet felt cold as I shivered, and then I opened the door as I caught my breath.

Chapter Thirteen

Harriet said, "I thought your friend's mom was going to let you come home earlier."

I gulped and tried to think of another lie. I said, "Um, I was going to come home earlier, and then I got caught up in the new video game he was showing me. That's why I am home late."

Then I went to my room, shut the door and sat on my bed while looking at my window behind me.

I sensed my bedroom door open. I noticed the person's feet were a bit smaller than mine. It was just Daniel coming in.

I said, "Hey, are you okay, Danny?"

Daniel said, "Yes, Tom, I am okay. Harriet said it's time to eat."

I told Daniel, "I'm coming down in a minute."

Without another word, Daniel was already heading downstairs.

I swung my legs over my bed, and then I got up and started going down the stairs.

When I reached the bottom I was sleepy, but I forced myself to stay awake. Then I turned to the kitchen, where Dad, Harriet and Daniel were all eating mashed potatoes and peas with rice.

I looked down at my plate and started eating slowly. When I finished, I went to the office room, which was next door to the kitchen.

I grabbed my satchel bag to continue writing this essay project for English, and then I fell asleep. I didn't know how long I slept for while I was meant to be doing my homework.

Then I heard someone say, "Tommy, we are going to watch TV."

I turned around – my eyes were still sleepy. I noticed it was Daniel, and I said, "Soon, Daniel."

I went to the living, sat down, and we watched SpongeBob SquarePants.

I fell asleep, and then Daniel continued watching while Dad came and sat down on the opposite side of the couch while eating some grapes. Harriet and Dad started talking, which got on my nerves, so I told them, "I'm going to my room for a nap. Tell Daniel to wake me later."

Without another word, I went upstairs, went to my room and slept. Daniel came back to my room like he always does to wake me up. I groaned and turned over to my side, and then I opened one eye and saw Daniel by the door.

Then I swung my legs over, got up and went downstairs, where Harriet and Dad chatted about adult things I didn't like listening to.

I ate some more, and when I finished I went back to the living room to watch TV.

Daniel sat by me, watching the TV, and then I heard a knock on the door. I went to answer it, and Sarah was standing at the door, with her long brunette hair done up in a ponytail.

Chapter Fourteen

I invited Sarah inside and introduced her to Harriet, and then I went upstairs with her to my room.

Sarah looked around my room – it was her first time seeing it. "Tom, your room is pretty cool with the lights changing colour."

I smiled and replied, "Thank you, Sarah"

We both talked for a while, before Sarah said she was going home, so I went downstairs to see her off.

I closed the door and went back to my room, and then I went on my laptop and surfed around the internet.

After I was done looking around, I lay down for a bit. The next minute I was asleep again.

***

I woke up around noon, noticing the sky was dark grey, which meant it was going to rain. I forgot I had left my bike outside, so I rubbed my eyes and made sure I was fully awake, and then I put my coat on and went downstairs.

I ran to get my bike. The raining started pouring as I got it to the shed and put it away, and then I closed the door before I went inside the house.

By the time I got inside it was warm and cosy, as Harriet must have put the fireplace on ready for that night, which is going to be very cold.

I went up to my room and changed into my jumper, also putting on some sweatpants and socks.

Then I put the laptop on and started on my English exam paper. It was due this Tuesday, so I started writing a story I made up about having friends and hanging out together.

I finished it and lay back on my bed, looking at the ceiling and the light.

I went to Daniel's room to see if he was okay, and I saw him holding the book I didn't want him to touch. I asked him why he was touching the book and told him not to.

I took it from his hand, and then I went to my room and hid it in a place he wouldn't find it. Why didn't I want him to read it? I remember being a kid and adding memories of my mother, and every day I wrote it down, but when she died I didn't want anyone to read it, apart from myself.

Chapter Fifteen

Daniel looked at me, scratching his head, wanting to know why I was acting so strange. I told him not to go into my room or touch that book. If he did, he would be in trouble.

Daniel said nothing and went back to his room.

The house remained quiet, until I heard Dad sounding drunk again, fighting with Harriet after dinner. Dad refused to help her because he'd had two bottles of vodka.

Harriet kept quiet cleaned the table by herself. I went downstairs to help her. Harriet was still cleaning the coffee table. When I asked her to give me a cleaning cloth, she just threw it in my face without giving it to me nicely in my hands. I blinked at her slightly, feeling confused, and then I ignored her and started cleaning some of the windows.

When I finished, I went to my room and cleaned up the mess. I did this while doing my homework assignment, took out a few old toys and put them in Daniel's room, thinking of how I'd hidden the book somewhere no one would find it.

Then I went downstairs and sat down on the sofa, reading a book. I heard Daniel trying to get the book from my room, and I shouted, "Daniel! What are you doing?"

Daniel looked at me in shock and said, "Nothing, Tom. I wanted a toy to play with."

I took my stepladder and got the toy down for him, and then I went back downstairs to watch TV. I heard someone at the door.

I said, "Hello, Sarah?"

Sarah smiled at me. "Hello, Tom."

I invited her in and we talked for a while, and then Sarah said, "Your house is pretty quiet, isn't it?"

Chapter Sixteen

I nodded yes because the others were asleep. I pointed them out to her, apart from Daniel, who waved from the stairs.

Sarah laughed and waved back at Daniel as she went upstairs, giving him a high five, and then she and Daniel came back down. Sarah and I went outside, but we left the door open for Daniel if he wanted to join us.

Daniel came to us, so Sarah looked at me and asked if we could all go to the cinema together.

I nodded, and then I said to Sarah, "Daniel and I are going to change now."

Sarah smiled and waited in the living room for us while she texted her friends on her phone.

When we were done, Sarah stood up all ready to go, and she said, "I told Harriet we are going to the cinema. She said it was okay."

Then we all walked down to Great Movie World. This was the best cinema in Northern Hills. We got to the entrance and paid two dollars for our tickets. Before it was five dollars, so they had made it cheaper.

We had to plan what we were going to watch, which was a hard decision to make. We got our heads down together and I suggested *Transformers*. Sarah said *Capture the Flag*, and Daniel agreed with her.

I sighed and said, "*Capture the Flag* it is, then."

Daniel and Sarah both smiled, and we all went inside to watch *Capture the Flag*.

Chapter Seventeen

While we were watching the movie, I got up and went to the bathroom. When I came back, the movie was almost halfway through.

Sarah got up and she went to the bathroom as well, while I sat by her seat and kept Daniel company.

Sarah finally came out. I asked her what took her so long, adding that Daniel wanted the bathroom too. She said, "Oh, okay, right," in a sad voice.

I asked if there was something wrong. She shook her head and looked at the floor, not making eye contact with me.

Daniel said, "I'm going to the bathroom." It was just Sarah and me now, waiting for him.

I looked around, while Sarah looked curiously at me. I heard her start mumbling, but she stopped when she met my eyes.

Sarah sighed and spoke about her brother, Caleb, who was always in trouble at school for his anger issues and stubbornness.

My eyes changed colour as the lights turned back on – they went light brown instead of dark. As Sarah looked at them, I turned to her and asked, "Why are you looking at me like that?"

She replied, "I've never seen your eyes change colour before."

Daniel came out of the bathroom, and said, "Did I take long?"

I responded, "No, Daniel, you didn't take long, but I'm hungry now."

We all got our coats together and started to leave like everyone else. It was quite cold leaving the cinema, so I quickly got my coat on, as did Daniel and Sarah. The worst part was that it started to rain, so we all started running.

Chapter Eighteen

I slipped in a puddle and shouted, "HELP!"

Sarah stopped running. Daniel came closer to me and asked if I was okay.

I winced in pain and said, "No, I'm not, ugh."

Daniel quickly grabbed my phone and gave it to Sarah to call an ambulance. Sarah told them I was bleeding and that I was in pain.

The operator said, "I'll send them out now."

We started to hear the siren as they parked by us – we were standing by a house. The paramedics got out of the car.

Then both Daniel and Sarah explained to them what had happened.

One of the paramedics asked if I was all right. I told her no, feeling the blood from the side of my stomach pouring into my hand and jacket.

The paramedics gently helped me up and took me into the ambulance. As Daniel and Sarah watched me go inside, Sarah found Harriet's number on my phone and rang the house.

She explained to Harriet, "Tommy is badly hurt. The ambulance is going to take him to hospital so he won't be home."

Harriet said, "All right – make sure Daniel is okay, because it's getting cold and dark now."

Chapter Nineteen

The ambulance left as Daniel and Sarah started walking down the road to go home. Daniel said, "Is Tommy going to be okay? I mean, I don't like how he is at times, but I do love him. He is my brother."

Sarah sighed before answering. "I don't know, Daniel. He seems badly hurt."

Sarah and Daniel both got to the house and Harriet let them in. Sarah started to explain with Daniel what happened to me, and Dad looked as worried as Harriet was.

Daniel said, "What are we going to do, Dad? What if Tommy doesn't come back alive?"

"Now, Daniel," said Dad, "I don't think anything serious will happen. Tommy will be all right."

Harriet said, "But Adrian, we need to go to the hospital and watch him to see if he'll be all right." She looked at the floor, feeling bad for how she had treated me.

Dad looked at Harriet. "Is there something wrong?"

Harriet said, "No, I am fine," as she started thinking again.

Sarah said to Dad, "I need to go home now – it's late and I need my dinner."

Dad thanked Sarah for telling them what had happened and for bringing Daniel home, as Sarah opened the door and left. Meanwhile, the three of them didn't feel comfortable about me and wanted to go to the hospital, but it was nine p.m. and it was dark outside.

Dad said, "We'll go and see him tomorrow."

Daniel went upstairs to get ready for bed. It didn't feel the same without me. My bedroom felt dusty and cold as he stood and watched, while tears came to his eyes. He went to his room and got into bed, wishing Sunday morning would be here so he could see me in hospital.

Chapter Twenty

Sunday morning came just as he'd wished. He woke up and went to the bathroom to brush his teeth and have a shower. Harriet and Dad had already brushed their teeth and showered, and were sitting at the kitchen table eating breakfast.

Harriet shouted, "Daniel! Your breakfast is going to be cold, so hurry up!"

Daniel shouted, "I am hurrying as fast as I can, okay?"

He went to his room and got dressed in his Mickey Mouse t-shirt, dark skinny jeans, and some green Converse, and he ran downstairs as he was told to so he could hurry for his breakfast.

Daniel sat down and ate his Coco Pops, while Dad and Harriet thought about how badly hurt I was and how they had both treated me.

Daniel heard a knock on the door and opened it. "Oh, hi, Caleb. You know Tommy is hurt, right? And where is your sister?" he said.

Caleb saw Daniel and started laughing. He said, "Oh, hi, Danny. Yeah, I did know. Tommy is in my grade, and my sister is catching me up now. You're the seven-year-old boy who wears Mickey Mouse still." He started laughing.

Sarah beat Caleb in the arm and said, "Don't make fun of Daniel like that. You know what's going to happen when Tommy finds out."

Caleb said, "Oww! Didn't have to hit me that hard! And who cares what Tommy's going to do?"

Sarah sighed and asked, "Are you all right, Daniel? Are you ready to go and see Tommy?"

Daniel said, "Yeah, I am all right, Sarah. And yeah, I am ready to see him today."

Caleb stayed quiet as he followed his sister inside with Daniel. Dad and Harriet were all set for Daniel and Sarah to go to the hospital.

Sarah said, "This Caleb, my sixteen-year-old brother. I told him to watch your house while we're gone."

Dad smiled and said to Sarah, "That's totally fine by me." He looked at Harriet for agreement, and Harriet nodded.

Caleb said, "Bye. I hope you all will be okay."

They all got into the car, and Dad drove them to Great Northern Street Hospital where I was admitted.

Dad drove to the car park and parked in a space before they all got out.

Daniel said, "I need the toilet. I'm bursting," as he looked at his dad.

Dad said, "Let's go inside, everyone, and then you can use the toilet, Daniel."

They all went inside – there weren't many people around. Dad and Daniel went to the men's bathroom, as Sarah and Harriet sat down and waited for them.

Sarah said, "Tommy told me a lot about you, Harriet. So are you his new mother?"

Harriet looked at Sarah in surprise. She said, "Yes, I am, Sarah, since his real mother died."

Dad and Daniel came out of the bathroom, and Dad asked the nurse where I was. The nurse said, "Blue Wing, second floor."

They took the lift to Blue Wing, which was on the second floor. The ward looked like it was underwater and has bright glass windows.

They met my doctor, Harris Taylor, and they all shook his hand. He showed them to my ward, where I was half-awake when I saw everyone. I was happy and hugged Daniel, and smiled when I saw Sarah.

Sarah said, "How are you, Tommy? And is your stomach okay?"

I said, "I am okay. My stomach is stitched up and it hurts a little, but I am now recovering."

Dad and Harriet both said, "Tommy, you're okay. We were very worried. How is your side of your stomach?"

I told them both, "I am fine, but I can't walk or eat yet since I am still recovering."

They all stayed with me for a while, until it was dark and I started to feel sleepy. I said, "It's pretty late and I am a bit tired now," as I hugged Daniel goodbye and waved to everyone.

They all waved goodbye back and got into the car. Sarah called Caleb to say they were coming home so he should stand by the door for them.

Caleb was by the door in his jacket, barefoot, as my dad parked on the driveway. They got out of the car and went inside. Caleb was now in the living room waiting for them.

Sarah said, "Caleb, were going home now."

Caleb said, "Ugh, okay. See you, Mr Dawson and Mrs Robinson." The door shut behind them.

Daniel took off his jacket and sat down in the living room to watch TV. He said, "There was a razor on the floor. I think when Tommy slipped, the razor cut his jacket and went into the side of his stomach. It was really sharp and was a few inches long."

Dad and Harriet looked at Daniel in shock, and then Harriet said, "Oh, my. Tommy was really bleeding – that's a really sharp razor."

Dad nodded and said, "I'm sure he'll be all right. I hope he will be. He also went through the pain of losing his mother."

Chapter Twenty-One

Harriet nodded, sighed, and said, "But I treated him badly, and I want us to get along."

At that, the phone started ringing, and Harriet answered it. It was the hospital. Harriet said, "Doctor Harris, is Tommy okay? Did he recover?"

Doctor Harris went quiet and said, "Tommy is slowly improving, but the recovery isn't really good right now – he's been throwing up a lot, so we're going to operate on him again to see if he benefits from it."

Harriet sighed and said, "Thank you, Doctor Harris. I hope everything will be okay, and tell Tommy that we love him and hope he recovers well."

Doctor Harris said, "I'll tell him that, and thank you for your time, Mrs Robinson," before he hung up.

Harriet came and sat down, shaking her head, and said, "Boys, it wasn't good news." She sighed, stroking Daniel's hair.

Daniel looked at his father and then at Harriet. "So is Tommy going to be all right?"

Dad sighed and said, "I don't know, Daniel, but let's hope he will be."

Harriet sat down and thought about how she had treated me badly. It all flashed back into her head as she wiped her tears and pretended to be fine.

Daniel went to his room, and Dad went to grab another glass of beer.

***

Meanwhile, I was on the hospital bed. My head was spinning around in circles, and I started thinking how deep the razor had cut the side of my stomach. I started to mumble about how I was treated by Harriet, and then I heard a soft voice say, "Are you all right, Tommy? It's me, Doctor Harris."

I jumped and responded, "Yes, Doctor Harris," and then I looked down at the pillow.

Doctor Harris came next to me and said, "I know you're not all right, Tommy. You've been speaking to yourself a lot lately. Is there something bothering you? Sometimes I can hear you in my office."

I gulped. "No, Doctor Harris. I am fine, honest."

Doctor Harris stood up and said, "You can call one of the nurses if you need anything, Tommy. I'll be in my office, too, if you want something from me instead of the nurses."

I smiled at him and said, "Okay, Doctor Harris. I will."

When Doctor Harris left the room, I started playing on my Game Boy, and then I fell asleep for a while. When I woke up I wanted to use the toilet, but I couldn't get up from the pain.

I shouted, "Nurse Heidi! I want the bathroom."

She came over and said, "All right, Tommy, but I can't do it on my own. You're a little bit heavy." The other nurses came along and helped me to the bathroom.

Heidi opened the door and asked, "Tommy, do you want me to come in?"

I replied, "No, Nurse Heidi, I'm okay. I can manage."

"Okay, if you say so, Tommy. But that's what we're for – to help."

I felt my face turn red in the bathroom, as I couldn't pull my pants down, and the pee went down my legs. Then I was done, and I flushed the toilet, pretending I peed in it.

Heidi opened the door and said, "You lied to me, Tommy Dawson. Look at your pants. You smell like pee."

Other boys in my ward who were older than me started laughing, and younger girls and boys were also laughing. I went completely red and I wanted to cry, and then I did a little baby run back to my ward and sat on the chair by my bed, looking down at the floor.

Nurse Heidi came over and kneeled in front of me. She said, "Tommy, I'm sorry I was mad at you, and I didn't mean it, but you shouldn't have lied to me like that."

I looked at her as tears ran down my cheeks. "I was embarrassed – plus, I've never had anyone see my down below before, and I wanted to do it myself. I'm sorry I lied to you."

Heidi looked at me and laughed. "Oh, Tommy, there is nothing to be embarrassed about. We wouldn't tell anyone a thing about your body, and we care a lot about young boys like you. I have a son around your age – his name is Connor."

I laughed and smiled at Heidi, and I asked her, "Is Connor the boy who is a bit shy around people?"

Heidi nodded. "Yeah, that's him. I can call him over to speak with you."

I shrugged and said, "Okay, then – that would be cool."

Heidi got up and went to find him. She came back with Connor, and left us both to talk.

Connor was shy, and he was shaking with nerves because he had never met me before. Then he said, "Hi, I'm Connor – Heidi's son."

I responded, "Hello, I'm Tommy. Your mom helped me out to the bathroom."

Connor said, "Oh, yeah, she's told me a lot about you. But I was too shy to come closer to you – I tend to help her look after the younger kids in this ward."

"Oh, really? That's awesome – you must be good at watching the kids."

He chuckled. "It's not easy watching them. So how old are you, Tommy?"

"I'm thirteen now and I'll be fourteen next year, but I'm not looking forward to it."

Connor looked shocked. "Oh, why not, Tommy?" he asked. "Fourteen is a cool age – I am almost sixteen."

I sighed. "I don't like my dad's ideas, and I don't have any friends in my area, apart from Sarah."

Connor went quiet. "Oh, I see. Don't worry, Tommy. I would come to your party, if my mom allows me to, and I'm sure she will, because she likes you a lot. She says you're so adorable."

My face went red. I tried to cover it, so Connor wouldn't see me blushing.

Connor looked at what I was doing to my face. "Aw! Tommy, you're blushing," he said, and chuckled lightly.

"No! I'm not blushing now." I removed my hands from my face.

Heidi came back and said to Connor, "Blake wants the bathroom."

Connor groaned and said, "Ugh, Mom, do I have to now?"

I chuckled and said to Connor, "He is the youngest boy in this ward – what if you had a brother his age, Connor? His sister Alice can't take him – she's a girl, and she is eleven."

Heidi sighed at her son and said, "Tommy is right, Connor – Blake is young, and Alice is only eleven, so she can't take him."

Connor also sighed. "All right, since Tommy said he is the youngest – but Blake so annoying for a six-year-old. Every minute he wants something." He got up and went to the children's ward – the hall next to me – and I saw him taking Blake to the boys' bathroom.

***

Daniel came home from school and asked his dad, "Did Tommy call today, Dad?"

Dad said, "No not yet – I believe he is busy on his Game Boy."

Daniel put his bag down as he sat on the sofa. "Tommy is always addicted to his Game Boy," he giggled.

Dad laughed and asked, "So how was school today?"

Daniel replied, "School was fine. Students and teachers from Tommy's class hope he is okay, and that he recovers well."

Harriet came over and said, "Oh, Daniel – you're home now. So how was school today? Your dad must have told you Tommy hasn't rung yet."

Dad laughed, looking at Harriet, and told her what Daniel had just said.

Harriet nodded her head and smiled. "Aw, that's really sweet of them, Daniel."

Daniel shrugged his shoulders. "Yes, I guess it is," he said, and started giggling again.

***

Meanwhile, I was on my Game Boy again, just as my dad imagined me doing, when I saw Connor coming back to me, after he was done helping Blake.

Connor looked at me, amazed, and said "You have a Game Boy! I mean, I love Game Boy too, but my mom wouldn't get me one. She says they cost a lot of money, but I want one for my sixteenth birthday."

I laughed, looking at his amazed face. "I had this Game Boy when I was five years old. I really wanted one, so I remember crying and begging for one. My mom got it for me."

Chapter Twenty-Two

"She passed away when I was eight, so I lived with my dad and my brother alone."

I felt a pool of tears come to my eyes, and I looked down at the floor.

Connor came over and hugged me. "Wow, that's really sad. I felt it in your eyes that you're upset. I know how you feel – I used to have a sister, but she died from a bike accident when I was two years old."

I nodded and looked up at him. "Wow, that's so sad. I'm glad you understand how I feel, because my stepmother doesn't."

We both talked for a while. I began to like Connor – he felt like an older brother to me, and he had been through so much for a fifteen-year-old. Even though I am thirteen, there was something we had in common.

"Connor – Nick Bailey." It was one of the nurses, and she said, "Your mother needs you to help her in the children's ward."

Connor got up and said to me, "Tommy, I loved our conversation, but I must get back to being the children's ward assistant now. I'll catch you up later."

I said, "All right, Connor – see you later."

As I saw him leave with the nurse, heading for the children's ward on my right, I wondered what being a children's ward assistant was like. From the way Connor explained it, I believed it was not an easy job.

I saw Connor going to the boy's bathroom, and then he came over to me after. "I am on my break now," he said, "so we can talk for a little while."

I asked him, "What does a children's ward assistant do?"

Connor explained, "I help out with the younger children if there aren't enough nurses around, and if the children need to use the toilet or eat. I help the boys as my mom helps the girls, because girls don't like to be seen by boys."

Chapter Twenty-Three

I listened and nodded. "Wow, Connor, but you do a really good job at it. Do you want to work in a children's ward one day?"

Connor laughed and said, "Yeah, why not? It can be annoying sometimes, running back and forth, but since my mom works here I can't stay home and let her do the work, since I live with my stepdad. He isn't a great guy to be around. He always keeps doing drugs, and I don't want to talk about the rest."

I nodded, looking at him, I said, "Oh, wow. That's a real struggle, and aw, that's nice that you like helping your mom in the children's ward." I laughed. "Yeah, it doesn't sound easy, but it's worth it."

Connor nodded and chuckled. "Yeah. I'd better get back to work, or the nurses will find me still here."

I said, "Okay, Connor. I will see you later when you're free."

After he left, I tried to get myself onto the bed, since I was tired, and then I wrapped myself in the sheets and fell asleep.

***

Daniel had his dinner, and then he went upstairs to get ready for bed. He sneaked into my room and grabbed the book. He didn't want me to see. When he opened it, all the memories we had with our mother appeared before his eyes.

He then closed the book, put it back on the shelf, ran to his room and fell asleep.

***

I called the house phone to see if Daniel was asleep, since he had school the following day, and to tell Harriet and Dad I'd be coming home the following Monday. Doctor Harris said I was well enough to go home and back to school.

The house phone rang, and my dad picked it up.

"Hi, Dad. How are you?" I said.

My dad responded, "Hello, Tommy. I am good – we all miss you a lot, especially Daniel."

I said, "Aw, I miss you all too. I made a friend here as well. His name is Connor, but he's not with me now – he's on duty. I am coming home on Monday, as Doctor Harris thinks the wound has healed enough now for me to walk and be independent again."

Dad said, "Oh, really? That's cool. I hope I meet your new friend too."

We both laughed and talked for a while. Harriet wanted to speak with me too, and said, "I'm glad you're doing well, Tom, and I hope I meet your new friend, Connor, too. Sarah has been around here quite a lot after what happened."

I responded, "Oh, aw, that's nice of her. I am going to sleep now, so I'll see you on Monday."

Harriet said, "Okay, then, Tom. Goodnight, and see you on Monday."

I got up and went to the bathroom to use the toilet. After I was done, I went back to my bed, put my phone down and fell asleep.

***

When I woke up on Monday, Connor came over to see if I was okay, and I had breakfast. I said to him, "I am going to miss you, buddy, since I am going home today."

Connor looked at me and said, "I'll miss you too, but I don't live far from you, so maybe I'll come and visit when you're home." He smiled, but he felt a bit sad that I was going, since we were good friends, so he gave me a hug as a goodbye.

I went to Doctor Harris' office and he said, "Aw, Tommy – you're leaving the ward today. Remember what I told you about the wound – cover it up before having a shower." He got up and gave me a hug, and gave me a sticker for being a good patient to him.

I gave him a little stuffed teddy. "This is yours, Doctor Harris, for being a good doctor to me, and for coming to see me every night."

Doctor Harris started laughing. "Oh, how sweet of you, Tommy. It will sit somewhere on my desk for me to remember you by."

I waved goodbye to him and I got to the hospital stairs. Once I got downstairs, I went to reception and waited for Dad to pick me up. I waited for an hour before I saw the car park up in the driveway, and then I saw Dad coming out of the car. I took my suitcase and backpack and stood by the reception door for him to see me.

Dad said, "Aw, Tom! I'm glad you're coming home – I've missed you!"

I smiled and said, "I missed you too, Dad. Doctor Harris said I shouldn't do too much to affect the wound."

Dad put my stuff in the back, while I sat in the front passenger seat and put my seatbelt on. When we got to the house, Dad got my stuff out and quickly went inside. I felt confused, and I turned on the lights.

"SURPRISE! WELCOME HOME, TOMMY!"

"You all did this for me," I said.

Daniel said, "Of course we did. I'm so happy you're home."

Sarah laughed and said, "We all missed you, Tommy – even I did."

I said, "I don't even know what to say."

The welcome home party was so much fun. We all played games, and then Dad said I should tell them how it all went at the hospital, about how I am better but I should cover up my wound when I have a shower.

The party went on. I whispered to Sarah to come outside and she followed me. We both stood on a small hill watching shooting stars.

I looked at Sarah and I had to admit it – she was pretty, with long brown hair that fell to her shoulders, brown eyes that twinkled like stars, and her cute floral clothing.

I wrapped my arm around her and said, "You're so amazing, Sarah, and I don't know how to say thank you for helping me."

Sarah's face went red. With tears in her eyes, she said, "Aw! Tommy, you don't have to thank me. I am glad to be your friend and help you."

Daniel said, "Tommy, it's getting late, and Harriet wants you inside now."

Sarah replied, "I have to go home too, Tommy – I'll meet you after school, if you go tomorrow."

I shouted to her, "Maybe I'll go to school tomorrow!"

Then Sarah went home and I went inside with Daniel. The party was over and Harriet and Dad were watching TV on the sofa.

Daniel started to feel sleepy – I knew when I looked in his eyes – so I took him by the hand and said to Harriet, "I'm taking Daniel to bed."

Harriet said, "Okay, Tommy, but it's your bedtime as well."

I said, "Okay, Harriet, I will go to bed. I'll go to my room after I've stayed with Daniel for a while." I'd been in the hospital for so long that my sleeping pattern had been so weird, so I had to lie to her.

Harriet said, "Okay, I'll be coming upstairs to check, Mr Dawson, if you're in bed."

I said goodnight to Daniel, ran to my room and got myself into bed, pretending to be asleep, just in case Harriet came to check my room, as I knew she would tell my dad that I wasn't asleep.

Harriet came to my room to check if I was asleep. I pretended I was, and then she left the room. I felt sleepy as my eyes began to close.

Soon I was fast asleep, but then I sensed a light come through to my room. I put myself under the covers to block it, and I heard a voice.

"Tommy, wake up. I can't sleep."

I sensed the mystery person come to my bed, and they said again, "Tommy, wake up. I can't sleep."

I opened one eye, still tired, and said, "Daniel? What are you doing in my room? It's five in the morning, dude."

Daniel said, "But I can't sleep. I had a bad dream – I was being chased by a monster."

I got up and sat by him. "There are no monsters, Daniel – it must have been your imagination."

Daniel looked at the floor, and tears came down from his eyes.

"Is there something wrong? You've never been this quiet before," I said.

Daniel said, "No, there's nothing wrong, Tommy. I am fine."

I said, "Daniel, I am going to sleep now. Are you going to your room, or do you want to sleep with me for the night?"

"I'll sleep with you," Daniel said, as he got under the covers. I turned off my lamp, and we both started sleeping.

***

The sun shone through my window. I heard the door open, and Harriet came in. She said, "Boys, wake up – you have school today." Then she started shaking us both to wake up.

Daniel woke up and said, "It's morning already? Do I have to go to school today?"

Harriet said, "You have to, Daniel, or your teacher will call and ask me."

Daniel sighed and did as he was told, getting down from the bed. He went to brush his teeth as I stayed sleeping.

Harriet knew I was harder to wake up than Daniel. She pulled the covers and sheets like Dad does, and I said, "Ugh! Do I have to wake up now? Just a few minutes, please?"

"Tommy Charles Dawson! You need to wake up now, young man!"

I got up then. I slammed the door hard and walked to the bathroom. There I brushed my teeth, and after that I got in the shower. When I was done, I went to my room and got dressed in my school uniform, and then I went downstairs and sat on the sofa.

Dad said, "Tommy, come here, please." I ignored him, so he said it again. "Tommy Charles Dawson, I know you heard me."

I felt my anger rise even more, and I took my bag, opened the door and slammed it. I walked down to the bus stop feeling angry.

Daniel said, "I've never seen Tommy that angry," as he got his bag, and then he said bye, closed the door and met me at the bus stop.

Daniel said, "Tommy, are you okay? You were really angry this morning."

I said to Daniel, "I'm not really in a good mood to talk now."

The bus came. Daniel went in and asked me, "Are you coming on the bus, Tommy?"

I said to Daniel, "Not today. I'm sorry, buddy – I'm going to walk instead. Don't feel like taking the bus."

Daniel said, "All right, Tom. See you later, then – bye."

I waved bye back at Daniel as the doors closed, and then the bus took off to Daniel's school.

I got my bag over my shoulder and started walking to school. I kicked a stone and started thinking about how I hated being told what to do by my stepmother. Dad always agreed with her and let her treat me like a two-year-old, even though I am not.

Everyone at school laughed at me, because they know Harriet liked to drop at the gate and kiss me on the cheek, and would give me a toy like a two-year-old boy going to kindergarten.

I got to the school and rushed to my first morning lesson. Boys and girls who were older than me started pointing and laughing with their friends. I wasn't in the mood – I ignored everyone.

I went to class and opened the door. Then my math teacher said, "Mr Dawson, wait outside, NOW!"

I closed the door and waited.

My teacher came out and said, "Look at the time you got here."

I looked down at my watch and stayed quiet. I knew I was late and I was in trouble.

My teacher said, "Class, it's break time now." The class started running outside for break, laughing at me continuously after they left.

Mr Gibson, my math teacher, called me and said, "Mr Dawson, come in and sit down."

I went in and stood in the corner, looking down at the floor.

Mr Gibson repeated what he said. "Mr Dawson, sit down, please."

I walked over to my seat and sat down angrily. I put my bag down, ducking my head.

Mr Gibson said, "You know what you're here for, right, Tommy Dawson?"

I said, "Yes, I do, because I was late."

"Since you're always late for my math lessons, I'm going to call your parents for a meeting about this."

"I'm going to the toilet," I said, getting up.

Mr Gibson said, "You are not allowed to go to the toilet now, Mr Dawson." He pointed to my seat for me to sit back down, but instead I opened the door and ran down the hall. Mr Gibson came out to find where I ran off to, but he couldn't see me anywhere, so he rang the principal to call my parents to come in.

I came out from the boys' toilets, and then I heard the loudspeaker: "TOMMY CHARLES DAWSON, COME TO THE PRINCIPAL'S OFFICE, NOW!"

It was Anna Johnson, our school principal. I walked down to her office and opened the door. Dad, Harriet, and Daniel were there, along with Mr Gibson.

Mrs Johnson said, "Tommy, I've known you since kindergarten – I used to be your teacher, so why are you showing up late for your lessons, and running around the corridor? That's not the Tommy I know."

I went quiet. "I don't know, Mrs Johnson."

I started playing with my fingers, looking down at the floor, and then Harriet turned to me and said, "So, Tommy, is this true? I'm really disappointed in you."

Dad said, "Tommy, I thought you could do better than that – I know you love math, so why do you behave like this?"

Mrs Johnson said, "Tommy, if this happens again there'll be more trouble. Do you understand me, young man?"

I said, "Yes, Mrs Johnson."

So I went with Daniel and my parents to the car, where it was very quiet inside. Then I said, "Harriet, can I use the toilet, please?"

Harriet said, "Tommy, you have to wait until we get home. I am not happy with you."

Daniel started playing his game. He didn't even look at me.

I said, "Dad, can I use the bathroom, please? I can't wait any more."

Dad said, "As Harriet said, you have to wait until we get home. I can't stop because I am in traffic."

I stamped my feet and groaned, and then I grabbed my stomach because I felt sick, and I felt a lump rising inside my throat. Before I could say that I wanted the bathroom again, I vomited on the car floor.

Harriet turned to the back to see what was going on. She said, "Adrian, park the car for a minute." She got out and told me to get out as she explained to Dad, "Tommy threw up in the back, so I need him to change into some clean clothes."

Dad looked at me and said, "There's a bathroom not far from the nursery."

We went to one of the bathrooms, and then Harriet gave me some clean clothes. I went to the boys' toilets to get changed.

After I was done, I came out and said, "I'm okay – a bit better now."

Harriet said, "I'm sorry we didn't let you use the bathroom – I didn't know you felt unwell."

I told her, "It's all right. I didn't know I would throw up that badly."

As we both walked back to the car, Dad cleaned up my vomit beneath my seat, and I got in the back again with Daniel.

When we were back home, Dad parked up the driveway, and I opened my door got out. Since I had a key, I went inside and sat down in the living room.

Harriet said, "Go to your room, Tommy, or there'll be time out."

I stood there and didn't move. I said, "I'm not going to my room, and you can't make me."

Chapter Twenty-Four

Dad came over and grabbed me. "Tommy Charles Dawson, go to your room, NOW!"

I said, "You're the worst father ever, and Harriet is the worst stepmother ever! I HATE THIS HOUSE!"

I ran upstairs to my room and slammed the door. I sat in the little corner that wasn't far from my door and cried.

Daniel went to his room and played on his Game Boy. Meanwhile, I heard a knock on my door.

"Tommy – it's Harriet. Should I come in?"

I said, "No, you can't come in! Go away!"

"Tommy, open this door. I need a word with you."

I thought about this for a moment, and then I said, "The door is open."

Harriet came in and knelt down in front of me. "Tommy, listen. Look at me. I know you're upset about how we've been treating you, but it not my fault, and it's not your dad's."

I said, "You have always said this to me, but you treat me like a two-year-old in front of Daniel, and you're rude to me." I felt tears run down my cheeks, and I looked down at the floor. I had memories of me and my mom and how she treated me. Harriet treats me like I don't exist to her.

"I want to be alone, Harriet," I said.

Harriet said, "Oh, right, then, Tom." I watched her take some of my clothes as she closed my door behind her.

I wrapped myself in my blanket and hugged my knees while I put my head down. Then I heard Daniel come in, and he said, "Tommy, are you all right?"

I said, "Yeah, I'm okay. I just wanted some alone time."

Daniel said, "Oh, I see. That's good that you're okay now." He smiled, showing a gap between his teeth.

I laughed and smiled at Daniel. Sometimes I'd remember how small my brother was back then. He has grown so much. His facial features are like mine, and his hair is dark brunette. My hair is light brunette, while his eyes are light brown, and mine are dark brown.

Harriet shouted upstairs, "Boys, it's time for dinner!"

Daniel said, "I'm coming!" He ran out of my room started going downstairs.

I got up and followed him downstairs, where I sat down next to him.

We both started eating, and then I said to him, "Daniel, you have finished eating so early."

Daniel said, "Yes, I have. I'm going to play outside in the rain."

Before I could say another word, Daniel was already outside. I shouted to him, "Daniel! Come inside or you'll catch a cold!"

Daniel replied, "Tommy, do I have to? I am having so much fun!"

I felt my feet slip as I grabbed the door to keep my balance.

Daniel saw me and ran over. "Are you okay, Tommy? You almost slipped."

I said, "Yes, I am okay – I slipped because of the wet edge on the floor." I went to the living room with Daniel, sitting down before him.

Harriet said, "Daniel Oscar Dawson, it's time for you to go to bed."

Daniel said, "But Harriet, it's still early and I don't want to sleep now."

Harriet said, "Daniel Oscar Dawson, you know you have an appointment tomorrow before school for your teeth."

I replied, "Oh, yeah, because you had a cavity in your back teeth, Daniel – remember?"

Daniel responded, "Oh, I remember now – I'll go to bed then."

I watched him go upstairs to his room, and the door closed. I looked at Dad, who was asleep on the couch to my left.

Harriet said, "Tommy, it's your bedtime too, since we have to go to Daniel's teeth appointment tomorrow."

I did as I was told. I went upstairs, undressed, and put my pyjamas on. After that, I went on my laptop and played a few games before bed.

I started yawning in the middle of the game, and I thought I should get some sleep. I got under the covers and turned off my lamp.

***

Wednesday morning came, and I woke up to get ready for school and Daniel's dental appointment. I went to the bathroom to brush my teeth and have a shower. After my shower I wrapped the towel around me, and I went into my room to change into my school uniform.

When I was fully dressed, the only thing that was annoying me was my school tie. I got my shoulder bag and went downstairs, while Daniel was still getting his jumper and school shirt on.

I sat down and had my breakfast, which was Coco Pops again. But I have my breakfast really light because of my stomach – when it's too heavy I feel sick. When I was done eating, Daniel was now fully dressed, and he sat down next to me to have his breakfast.

Chapter Twenty-Five

After Daniel finished eating, I got my shoulder bag, put my jacket on, and waited at the door for Harriet and Daniel.

They joined me at the door and we started walking to Northern Hills Children and Young People's Hospital.

We went inside and Harriet went to the front desk, while Daniel and I sat on the waiting chairs. When Harriet was done, she came and sat down with us.

I got up and looked around. I remember being in this hospital when I was eight because I hurt my knee, but the place looked more colourful and cleaner than it used to.

Then the doctor shouted, "Daniel Dawson!"

We all went into the office. I came in last, shut the door behind me, and sat down on one of the chairs.

The doctor introduced herself: "I am Helen Collins. So would you like to introduce yourselves to me?"

I said, "I'm Tommy Dawson, and I think I remember you from when I was eight."

Doctor Helen said, "Tommy, you have grown! I do remember you from when you broke your leg. You were a little eight-year-old boy." She gave me a hug. I hugged her back, since it had been a while since I last saw her.

She went back to Daniel and said to him, "Daniel, would you open your mouth for me, sweetie?"

Daniel opened his mouth as Doctor Helen looked inside, and then she said, "Everything looks fine in there, and the teeth have settled down, but the hole is a little bit big."

Daniel closed his mouth, and then said, "So my mouth is okay, Doctor Helen?"

Doctor Helen laughed and gave Daniel a sticker for being a brave patient.

She replied, "Yes, Daniel, sweetie – your mouth is fine."

After that, I gave Helen a hug and we left her office. When we went back to the entrance, the pharmacy gave Harriet medicine for Daniel's cavity.

I went outside and I started making my way, and then Harriet said, "Tommy, wait for us, please."

I ignored her because she always treats me like a two-year-old, and I am thirteen – I can go to school on my own. I ran to catch the bus, and then I got on, swiped my bus pass and sat down. I knew Harriet would be super mad now, but she had to take Daniel to school.

I always lied to her and said I took Daniel to school, but his bus showed up before mine, so mostly he went to school by himself, which he was not allowed to do yet.

I arrived at school and looked at my watch. It was 10.40 a.m. Since I started lessons at eleven, I had a few minutes to settle myself before my first class started.

I got off the bus, went through the school gate and sat down at the picnic table, playing on my Game Boy.

Then I heard someone shout, "Tom! You're back from hospital."

It was Lester – I had known him since kindergarten. I shouted to him, "I'm over here!" as I saw him coming over, and then he sat down.

Lester said, "How are you, Tom? I heard about your accident."

I said, "I'm doing okay, and yeah, it was quite bad. I couldn't do anything for a few days."

"Oh, wow – where is it, actually? Your whole side of your stomach, is it?"

"There's a plaster on it so it won't get infected, and yeah, it was the whole left side of my stomach."

Lester chuckled a bit and said, "Oh, man, that must have hurt when they operated and stitched it up."

I heard the bell and said, "Les, I've got class now – I'll catch you up later." Then I ran inside.

I looked down at my timetable. I had math again with Mr Gibson. I opened the door to my classroom and said, "Morning, Sir."

Mr Gibson said, "Morning, Tom. Get settled and have a seat."

I took off my jacket and put my bag down, and then I sat down with my pen and notebook out.

Mr Gibson said, "Morning, class. Today we are going to learn about addition. Does anyone know what addition means?"

One girl three rows behind me said, "Addition is about adding something together."

Mr Gibson said, "Almost, Brianna, but not quite what I am looking for. Anyone else?"

I raised my hand and said, "Adding a number to another number is addition."

Mr Gibson said, "Tom is right. As he said, adding a number to another number is addition."

Brianna said, "No! Tom is lying – how can you add another number and that's addition?"

I said, "No, I wasn't – I was right about what I said."

Brianna always thinks she's right. I felt my anger rise so much. I went over to her and said, "You always think you're smart, but I know more about math than you do!"

She laughed. "Oh, really, Tommy Dawson? What a surprise, but you know what? I don't care, because you're just a little wimp. Harriet stills treats you like a baby!" She was shouting by this point, and the whole class started laughing at me.

I took my stuff, walked out of the room, hid behind one of the lockers and cried.

Mr Gibson said, "Class, settle down now. I am coming back."

Mr Gibson came out into the corridor to find me, and then he saw my stuff behind one of the lockers. He came over to me and said, "Tom, are you okay? I'm sorry about them laughing at you. Do you want to go to Mrs Johnson?"

I sobbed and said, "Okay, sir." I took my stuff and went to Mrs Johnson's office.

The door opened. Mrs Johnson said, "Come in, Tom!"

I walked in and wiped my nose. Mrs Johnson said, "Are you okay, Tom?"

I said, "No, I'm not. Brianna and I had a fight, and she made the whole class laugh at me for how Harriet treats me like a kid."

Chapter Twenty-Six

Mrs Johnson said, "I'll have a word with Brianna, Tom. So do you want to go home? I know this isn't a great way to enjoy coming back."

I said to her, "I want to go home, Mrs Johnson." I put on my jacket and put my pen and notebook in my bag. "Bye, Mrs Johnson, and thank you."

I started walking down the corridor to the entrance door. I went down the stairs and walked to the bus stop.

The bus came and I got on, swiped my bus pass and sat down, looking out of the window. Harriet made everyone at school laugh and call me names.

Soon the bus stopped not far from my house. I got off and started walking home.

I took my key out from my pocket, opened the door and went inside. I went upstairs to my room and cried on my bed.

Harriet seemed worried, and I heard her coming up the stairs to my room. She said, "Tom, did something happen at school? Do you want to talk about it?"

I turned my head to the right side. "No, I don't want to talk about it."

Harriet placed her hand on my shoulder, which felt warm on my skin. "Tom, you never come home from school this early, and you never come straight to your room either. I'll leave you alone for a while, and then we must talk, okay?"

I said to her, "All right, then. Can I be alone now?"

Harriet said, "Yes, Tom, I'll leave you alone now, but later on we need a family meeting to talk about what's wrong with you today."

"Okay then. I'll be downstairs for lunch."

"Okay, Tom. I hope you feel better to talk soon." Then Harriet left the room and closed the door.

I turned to the left side of my pillow. As tears rolled down my cheeks, I started thinking about my mom, and how I wished she was here instead of Harriet. Since my stepmother took over, I never felt happy. I always felt like a two-year-old in front of Daniel and my friends.

I wanted to run away from home. I found a cloth to make a bindle, and I sneakily went into the bathroom, taking my toothbrush and toothpaste. I started packing all my things inside and tied it in a knot. I grabbed my jacket and, holding my bindle, opened my window to climb out.

It was dark, so I wouldn't be spotted by anyone. I started walking on. I was scared but I stayed brave and continued walking.

***

Harriet came into my room, went over to my bed, and pulled the sheets. Then she shouted, "Adrian! Have you seen Tom?"

Dad came to my room and said, "No, Harriet, I haven't."

Harriet looked in shock at the bed. "We have to find him – he could be hurt or lost right now."

Dad said, "I'm sure he'll be all right, Harriet – we'll keep a lookout."

***

I walked until I found the woods, and I went through. It was dark, with loads of scary bugs and animals around. I found some logs and decide to make a small fire.

After I made the fire, I sat on one of the logs and wrapped myself in a blanket.

***

Daniel came to the room and said, "What's happened? Where is Tom?"

Harriet said, "Your brother ran away and we're trying to find out where he went."

Daniel looked surprised. "No! How can this happen? We need to look for him."

Harriet grabbed the phone and rang the police. "Hello, I'm Harriet Robinson, and I'm speaking on behalf of my stepson, Tommy Dawson."

The policeman said, "Hello, Ms Robinson. Okay, what happened?"

Harriet explained to the policeman: "Tommy came home really early from school, and I was talking to him, and then he told me that he wanted some time alone. When I came back to his room to check on him, he was gone." She told him the address.

The policeman said, "I am going to send some police out to the house to look for him, Ms Robinson. My name is James, bye."

Harriet said, "Thank you, Officer James. Bye."

Daniel said, "Are they going to find him, Dad?"

Dad replied, "Of course, Daniel – they will."

There was a knock on the door. It was the police. Daniel ran downstairs and opened it, and he said, "My brother is gone – please find him, will you?"

The police woman said, "Aw! You're so adorable! So where are your parents, love?"

Chapter Twenty-Seven

Harriet came downstairs with Dad. "Hello, I'm Harriet, and this Adrian."

The policewoman said, "Hello, and nice to meet you both. I was sent here regarding a boy who has gone missing – is that right?"

Dad said, "Yes, it is."

The policewoman got out her notebook. "What's his name, and how old is he?"

Harriet said, "Tommy, and he is thirteen," as she looked worried.

The policewoman said, "Okay, what's his last name?"

Dad said, "Dawson."

"Does he have a brother?"

Harriet said, "Yes, that's Daniel."

The policewoman laughed and said, "Oh, aw! He was the one who opened the door."

Daniel went red when she said that, and he said, "You're welcome."

Then the policewoman said, "How tall is he? Do you know his height?"

Harriet and Adrian both said, "No, we don't know his height."

"Your house address is 24 Ally Street – is that right?"

Harriet said, "Yes, is it."

The police woman said, "Okay, so I have all the information you told me, and I am going with the other police officers to find him. Thank you, and bye."

Harriet said, "Thank you so much, and bye."

She closed the door and Dad said, "I think they'll find him."

Harriet went and sat down on the sofa, and then she said, "Why does Tom keep behaving like this? Doesn't he like home?"

Dad said, "It's because he feels he is thirteen now, so he should choose what he wants, and we treat him like a baby a lot."

Harriet said, "But Adrian, just imagine what could happen to him – although maybe you're right."

***

I was cold and hungry. I started thinking about why I ran away. I also needed the toilet, but there were none in the woods, so I crossed my legs and started wiggling around.

I heard a siren getting louder, and then I saw a flash of headlamps bright in my eyes.

The police in the car came out and said, "Are you Tommy Dawson?"

I said, "Yes, I am – what are you doing here?"

The policewoman said, "Right! Your parents sent us to look for you."

Then I said, "Are we going to the police station? Because I need the toilet."

She said, "Yes, we are. Okay, get in the car, Tom, and we'll keep you warm and dry at the station."

I got in the car and put on my seat belt. The policewoman started driving to the station. It wasn't a very long drive. Soon the policewoman opened my door and I got out.

I went inside, ran into the men's bathroom and did my business.

When I came out I felt a lot better, but I was hungry. The policewoman got me some lunch and sat next to me. She asked me some questions.

"Tom, do you get on with your parents? If you have a problem, you can tell me."

I said, "No, I don't get on with my stepmother, because my mom passed away when I was eight years old." I felt tears roll down my cheeks. "When I go to school, they make fun of me because of how my stepmother treats me."

The policewoman hugged me and said, "You're a strong boy – remember that, and ignore those at school who laugh. They don't know what you're going through. I might have a word with your stepmother about how she treats you, if you're happy with that."

I said, "Yes, I am – maybe you can change things around. You sound experienced – have you lost something you loved?"

"Yes, I lost my cat. Her name was Tokyo – I love the Japanese. She died when I was eleven and I never saw her again."

"Oh, wow. That's really sad."

"It's all right, Tom, but we need to get you home."

I finished my lunch while she asked me some more questions. Then I said, "Okay, so we are going now?"

She nodded.

I got my jacket on, held my bindle, and headed outside to the car. I sat down and put my seat belt on. I thought about how mad Harriet and Dad were going to be.

Finally, we got to the house, and the policewoman let me out of the car and followed me to the doorstep, where she knocked on the door.

Harriet answered it. She was in her nightgown and slippers.

The policewoman said, "I found him in the woods, wrapped up in a blanket."

75

Chapter Twenty-Eight

I looked down at the floor, realising how much trouble I was in.

The policewoman said, "I think you've got some explaining to do to your parents, Tommy Dawson."

I gulped and said, "Yes, I do."

We went inside. I went to sit down on the couch, while the policewoman had a word with Harriet in private. When they were done talking, they both came to the living room and sat down.

I explained why I ran away. "I didn't like being treated like a baby all the time, and I hated being told what to do."

Dad said, "Tommy, I know you can behave better than that. Harriet and I were worried – what if you got hurt, or someone took you away?"

I looked down at the floor. "I know, Dad, and I'm sorry."

Then Harriet said, "Thank you for finding him."

The policewoman said, "You are very welcome. Goodbye, Mrs Robinson."

The policewoman left, and Harriet shut the door.

I went upstairs to get ready for bed. I went past Daniel's room. He was already fast asleep.

I closed my bedroom door, took off my clothes, put my pyjamas on and got under the covers since I was tired. I didn't feel like playing a few games before bed.

Chapter Twenty-Nine

Morning came and it was Thursday. I was still fast asleep when I sensed a light come into my room again.

Then I heard, "Tommy, wake up! You're going to be late for dropping me off at the bus."

I groaned and said, "Daniel, just a few minutes, dude – it's only six a.m. and I am still not awake yet."

Daniel, Harriet and Dad are always the first three people up, and I am always asleep, so I wake up a bit late.

Daniel started shaking me to wake up. I didn't have a choice, so I got up and said, "Next time I am going to lock my door so that you don't come in until eight a.m. That's when I wake up – okay, Daniel?"

Daniel replied, "Yes, Tommy, I understand," as he left to go his room.

I went to the bathroom, brushed my teeth and had a shower. I wrapped the towel around me and went into my room to put my school uniform on.

After doing this, I needed the toilet so I went to use it. But, in general, I don't use the toilet in the morning, because everyone in this house uses it before me, and sometimes no one flushes the toilet, which makes me sick.

I went downstairs, and then I saw Daniel and Harriet in the living room, watching TV. Daniel was in his school uniform already. I had a feeling Dad went to work early.

Chapter Thirty

I sat down at the kitchen table, had breakfast really quickly, and then I got my shoulder bag on and put my house key in my pocket.

I used to have a phone, and then Daniel started playing a game on it. He took it to the bathroom and it dropped in the toilet. I was so mad at him that day, because I had that phone on my tenth birthday. I don't like my new phone as much.

I called Daniel over, took his hand and said, "Bye, Harriet," as I closed the door and started walking with him to the bus stop.

When we got there, Daniel started crossing his legs. I turned to him and asked, "Are you all right, Daniel?"

Daniel said, "No, I'm not, Tommy," as he looked down at his trousers.

I looked at his legs, which were gripped together. "Do you need the toilet, Daniel?"

Daniel said, "Yes, I'm bursting! I'm going to find somewhere to pee – can you hold my bag, Tom?"

I said, "Yeah, I'll hold it for you while you pee – the bus is not here yet."

I sat down on the bus stop bench, playing around with Daniel's school bag, until – *Oh no,* I thought – it was Caleb and his friends.

Caleb said, "Tom, you still take kids' stuff to school. I believe you are not thirteen – you are nine!"

One of the boys jeered, "You still like Mickey Mouse."

I gave them a dirty look, feeling my anger rise as I put the bags down. I stood really close to Caleb and said, "Who are you calling a nine-year-old?"

Caleb looked at me and said, "Who do you think you're messing with, Dawson?"

I punched him and kicked him in his knee. His friends tried to stop me, but I was too strong for them. Caleb punched me in the stomach, and I kneeled down, looking at the ground.

Caleb said, "Well, Dawson, I know you can never beat me."

The boys left me, laughing as they went to catch the bus to school.

I saw Daniel coming over after having his pee. He said, "Thank you for waiting," before adding, "Tommy, are you okay? Did something happen?"

I said, "When you left for your pee, Caleb came over with his friends. They started to make fun of me holding your school bag, and it turned into a fight."

Daniel said, "Oh, wow. Do you want to go home? You're bleeding."

I said, "Okay, Daniel, let's go home. I don't even want to go to school today." I got up as Daniel took my hand, and we started walking back to the house.

The door was open as Daniel and I went in. Harriet said, "Boys, you should be at school by now. Did something happen?"

I felt a bit of anger inside of me as I went into office room, picked up a book and threw it on the computer.

Then Harriet came in, grabbed me, pinned me down to the floor with her hands. She said, "Tom! Stop it now! If you want something, don't break anything in here!"

I said in anger, "LET GO OF ME, AND LEAVE ME ALONE!"

Harriet said, "Tom, calm down and tell me what happened."

I looked at Daniel, who was by the door. He said, "Tom, don't be angry. Calm down, please."

Tears rolled down my cheeks, and I said, "I had a fight with Caleb, Sarah's brother, about Daniel's school bag, and I got punched in the stomach."

"Oh, gosh," said Harriet. "Tom, get up and let me see your stomach. He might have even hurt your injury."

I got up and followed Harriet to the living room, while Daniel watched TV.

Harriet said, "Tom! Stand there. I am going to get your stomach plaster, and a cleanser for the wound."

I did as I was told and waited while my legs started aching.

Daniel saw me moving around and said, "Don't worry, Tommy – Harriet will be here now."

I said, "Harriet, I'm sitting down now, because my legs are aching."

"Okay," said Harriet, "just keep your top off for me, Tom."

I took my top off, which made me shiver, while I was sitting down by Daniel.

Finally, after what felt like two years of sitting by Daniel, Harriet came over with my stomach plaster and cleanser.

Harriet peeled off the old plaster, cleaned the wound and said, "It's getting better, and it's not as sore as before."

I screamed as the cleanser went into the wound, and I said, "It hurts, but I'm glad it's not sore anymore."

After Harriet cleaned the whole wound, she put a plaster on it and said, "This is so that it won't get any more infected, and it will heal quickly."

I put my top back on so that I wouldn't catch a cold, and I went upstairs to my room. I put my school clothes on the floor and went to my desk to do some drawing. Then I lay on my bed and fell asleep. After a while, Daniel came in.

He said, "Tom, do you want to play outside before dinner?"

I looked at him and groaned. "Daniel, let me get dressed first – I'll be downstairs in a minute, okay?"

Daniel responded, "Okay, Tommy – I'll be waiting on the sofa for you."

I found some clothes to wear and went downstairs while Daniel was waiting for me. Also, I heard Dad come back from work, and he said, "You didn't go to school, Tom?"

My stepmother added, "Tom, don't give your father excuses, because Daniel and I know why you didn't go to school today."

I said, "I had a fight with Caleb, Sarah's brother, because he made fun of me for holding Daniel's school bag."

My father sighed. "I think you and I have to go to the Wrights' house and speak with Sarah's parents about what happened."

I said, "Okay, Dad, but Daniel has to come with us, since we were going outside to play."

Daniel came over and took my hand. "Do we have to go to the Wrights' house?"

"Yes, Daniel, we have to go, so that Caleb won't mess with me again," I told him.

I sat on the step, put on my cherry red Converse and adjusted my trousers leg. Then I got up and put on my jacket so I was ready to go.

Daniel wasn't ready – he was still struggling with his shoes. I went over to him and sat him down on the sofa, helping him put on his navy blue Converse. I got his favourite rocket jacket and put it on him, along with his woolly hat and scarf so he wouldn't catch a cold.

Finally, Daniel and I waited for Dad. He couldn't find the house keys, and said, "Boys! You can make your way out, but wait for me outside."

I replied, "Okay – Daniel, let's make our way out before Dad comes."

I opened the door. Daniel and I walked down the path and stood outside the house gate. I looked at Daniel, and then I started laughing at how well I wrapped him up, because you can hardly see his nose or mouth in the entire scarf.

I saw Dad coming down to meet us, and he said, "Well done for waiting, boys! I thought you would have left without me, but you didn't."

I said, "It's all right, Dad – it wasn't a very long wait. Look how warm Daniel is in his scarf."

Daniel gave me a grin, and mumbled, "Thanks for making this my new fashion, Tommy," from under the scarf.

Dad started laughing. "Don't you worry, Daniel – I'll take it off when we get to the Wrights' house."

"Dad," I said, "will Harriet be okay in the house when we are gone?"

Dad looked at me and said, "We won't be very long in the Wrights' house, Tom, so I am sure Harriet will be perfectly fine."

Daniel and I ran to the bus stop and Dad followed behind us. He said, "Be careful, boys! Cars might be passing by."

Daniel and I stopped running and began to walk. We reached the bus stop. Dad came next to us and sat down on the bench with Daniel. I started crossing my legs, and I thought, *oh no, I forgot to use the toilet before we left the house.*

Dad said, "Are you cold, Tom? If you are then put your hands in your pocket."

I went over to Dad and Daniel with my legs crossed. I said to Dad, "I need the toilet – I am bursting."

Then Daniel said, "I need to go too, Dad."

Dad said, "The bus isn't here yet, so I'm giving you boys two minutes."

Daniel got off the bench and took my hand. We ran to find somewhere to pee while Dad was standing by the edge of the bus shelter, waiting for us.

Daniel and I went into one of the bushes and did our business. I zipped my pants and went over to help Daniel. After we were done, we both ran back to the bus stop. Dad had sat down by the time we got to him.

Dad said, "One bus has gone, but another one is coming in a few minutes. Boys, are you both okay now that you have peed?"

I said, "Yeah, we're okay now. I was really bursting – I was trying so hard not to pee myself."

Daniel said, "I am fine now too, and I agree with Tommy about that statement."

Dad and I both started laughing at Daniel's comment. Then I saw the bus coming, and I put my hand out for it to wait.

The bus stopped, the doors opened and everyone got out. We went inside and Daniel and I sat down. Then Dad swiped his bus pass and said to the driver, "Court Field Road Street, please."

The driver said, "Thank you very much."

Dad sat behind us and looked down at his phone while Daniel and I began drawing faces on the frosty window. It froze up our hands so we couldn't move our fingers.

Eventually, the bus stopped at Court Field Road Street, and I believed Sarah lived in one of these houses there. The bus doors opened and Daniel, Dad and I got off.

I saw Caleb outside, about to take out the trash. I said house 34 was where Sarah lived. I walked up to the front gate and asked Caleb, "Are your parents home? We're here because of you."

Caleb laughed. "Oh, really, Dawson? That's how tough you are? I think they're in."

Dad and Daniel followed me as I went inside. Also, I saw Sarah in her nightdress – she looked unwell but tried to be happy, and said, "Hello, Tommy. What brings you here?"

Dad said, "Sarah, I want to have a word with your parents."

Mr Wright said, "I am here, Mr Dawson – what is the problem?"

Dad said, "I'm concerned about how your son, Caleb, treated my son, Tommy, at the bus stop today."

I said, "Well, Mr Wright, it basically started when Daniel said he was going to pee, and I said okay. Then Caleb came over with his friends, and they started making fun of me for holding Daniel's school bag. It turned into a fight, and then Caleb punched me in the stomach, and I was bleeding really badly through my school uniform."

Mr Wright said, "This is not what Caleb should have done to you, Tommy. I'm really sorry about his behaviour, and I'll have a word with Caleb about that, okay? If you have any problems with Caleb then come to me, and I'll tell his mother about this incident as well."

Dad said, "Thank you, Mr Wright – we'll be going now. Bye."

Mr Wright waved to us and said, "Goodbye, Mr Dawson, and thank you."

I said, "I'm glad we came and sorted this all out, because Caleb always bullies me so his friends can laugh at me."

Dad said, "You won't be bullied any more. Since we've told his dad, I believe they'll give him a lesson."

Daniel said, "He totally won't bully you any more, or I'll get my sword on him and I will save the day."

I started laughing and said, "Daniel, everyone knows Star Wars swords are not real."

We went back to the bus stop. Daniel and I sat down on the bench, while Dad waited with the other people for the bus.

Dad put his hand out. The bus stopped and the doors opened. Daniel and I went to sit in the back.

Dad swiped his bus pass and said to the driver, "24 Ally Street is where we're getting off."

The bus driver said, "Thank you."

Then Dad found a seat in the front and sat down.

I had to put my hair to the side. It was so long, which made me feel so much like a girl. Then I thought to myself, *I really need a haircut this weekend*, but I couldn't be bothered to cut it.

Finally, the bus stopped at our street. Daniel, Dad and I got off the bus and started walking home.

Harriet was at the door. I ran to the gate and told her, "We sorted Caleb out. I ran because I am quite cold, and Dad and Daniel are catching up behind me."

Harriet said, "Okay, Tom – let me open the gate. I see your father and Daniel coming now."

She opened the gate and I went inside. Harriet followed, and then Dad and Daniel did too.

Daniel said, "Tommy, next time don't run and leave me and Dad walking."

Daniel was so worn out that his cheeks had turned red – that made Dad and I start laughing.

I took off my coat and shoes, and I stayed in my polka dot stripy socks. Then I went upstairs to my room and put on my t-shirt, which had a number twenty-three on it.

I went back downstairs and sat down in the living room with Daniel, watching Mickey Mouse with him.

Then I realised Daniel turned eight the following Monday, so we need to throw a party for him when he came home.

Daniel fell asleep on the sofa, while I changed the channel to one showing *Transformers*, which is my favourite show. I love watching it every afternoon.

I started to feel a bit sleepy, and then my stepmother said, "Tom, dinner will be ready soon."

I said, "Okay, Harriet. I will wake Daniel up."

I tapped Daniel on the shoulder. "Daniel, dinner will be ready soon."

Daniel woke up and said, "Okay then, Tommy."

I went over to the kitchen table. Harriet got out the plates and I sat down. Daniel came over and sat by me.

We started eating dinner. It was very quiet at the table, and then I heard the rain pouring outside. This caused our gate to make a lot of flapping and clapping noises.

After I was done having my dinner, I went upstairs to my room and got on my laptop. I surfed the internet for new games, found one and started playing it.

I fell asleep on my laptop, and when I heard the game alert, which meant someone had come online, it made me wake up.

I heard someone laugh, and I saw Daniel standing by my door. I asked him, "Danny, what's so funny?"

Daniel said, "Your sleeping on the laptop makes me laugh."

I laughed. "Oh, I fell asleep on my laptop again!"

Daniel went back to his room and played on his Game Boy.

I got ready for bed and changed into my pyjamas, and then I got into bed and fell asleep.

***

Monday morning came, and I woke up about six a.m. because it was Daniel's birthday. I sneaked into his room, but Daniel was still asleep. I tapped him on the shoulder, and he woke up and said, "What are you doing here, Tommy?"

I began to sing, "Happy birthday to you, happy birthday to you, happy birthday to Daniel, happy birthday to you." I gave him a hug and said, "Happy eighth birthday, buddy."

I gave him his birthday button to put on his school uniform.

Daniel said, "Thanks, Tommy. I am going to get dressed now, and then you can help me put the button on when I go downstairs."

I quickly went downstairs to check if Dad and Harriet had got Daniel's present ready before he came downstairs.

Harriet said, "Yes, Tom – it's all wrapped up in Daniel's favourite wrapping paper."

Daniel came downstairs and I helped him put on his birthday button.

I quickly went upstairs and, to get changed to my school uniform. When I was done getting dressed, I took the present I was giving to Daniel. I bought it when we went to the cinema, but in secret so no one would notice.

I went downstairs and put the present behind my back, so Daniel wouldn't see it until we had all sung to him.

Harriet and Dad sang together, "Happy birthday to you, happy birthday to Daniel, happy birthday to you," and, "How old are you now? How old are you now? Happy birthday to you!"

Daniel hugged them both and said, "Thank you so much."

We did a little prayer for Daniel, and Dad said, "Daniel, you are eight today, so I hope God makes you get everything you want today, and have a good birthday, amen."

We all said, "Amen, and thank you for blessing this family."

I got out my present from behind my back, which was a stuffed toy Mickey Mouse.

Dad and Harriet got him an iPad, since we all know Daniel loves his Game Boy, and we thought getting him an iPad would be more fun for him because he can play games on it.

Daniel was so happy that tears rolled down his cheeks, and then he hugged us all.

I said to him, "After school, we have a big surprise for you."

We sat down and had breakfast. After that, I brushed Daniel's hair – since it was his birthday, I wanted him to look very smart at school.

I got his new space jacket on, which was another present from all of us, plus a Converse school bag, which was navy blue.

I got my jacket and shoulder bag on, and we both said bye to Harriet and Dad. Then I opened the door and we started walking to the bus stop.

Daniel sat on the bench, looking down at his new watch I got for him.

I saw Caleb and his friends coming over, and I said, "What do you want?"

Caleb said, "Tommy, I wanted to apologise for how I behaved towards you on Thursday. I know it was wrong of me, punching you in the stomach. It won't happen again."

I thought about this, and then I said, "I accept your apology, and I'm sorry I got mad at you. My stomach is a bit better now."

Caleb stuck his hand out. "Friends?"

I did the same with my hand and we shook on it. "Friends."

We both started laughing together, and then Caleb said, "Who is the birthday boy?"

Daniel said, "The birthday boy is me. I am eight today, Caleb."

I started to chuckle. "Yes, you are, Daniel."

We all stood laughing and talking until the bus came. The doors opened and Daniel went in first.

I whispered in Caleb's ear, "Make sure you get ready for Daniel's party after school."

Caleb nodded at me.

I got on the bus, swiped my bus pass and sat down next to Daniel as the bus took us to my school first.

I pressed the stop button, saying to Daniel, "Enjoy school, buddy, and have a good day."

Daniel said, "Okay, Tommy – you too."

I waved bye at him as I got off, and he waved bye back at me.

I got to the school gate and looked down at my timetable. My first lesson was English, which I find the most boring out of all the subjects.

I went into room S02B, which was where my English class took place. I sat down, and then Miss Anderson came in – she was my English teacher.

She said, "Morning, class! Sorry I am late – I had to sort out an issue with one of our students."

The class groaned and said, "Morning, Miss Anderson."

Miss Anderson said, "Okay – today, we're going to learn about joining words together. Can anyone give me an example of what a joining word is?"

Before I opened my mouth to answer, Brianna said the answer before me. "A joining word is used to put words together."

I raised my hand and waited patiently.

Miss Anderson said, "Yes, Tom – do you want to answer the question?"

"Yes, Miss Anderson – a joining word is used in a group of words, and it makes a story, or a different way of saying a certain word."

Miss Anderson said, "Tom is almost right, but Brianna was correct. It means putting them together, but what Tom is saying is there too."

When the class was dismissed, I went to find Lester. He is my best friend, but he lives far away, so we only get to see each other at school. But I couldn't see him anywhere – I believed he hadn't come to school today.

Yes, I take my Game Boy to school, because I hated the silly things everyone does at break, like taking random pictures, spreading rumours and stuff like that. I am more of a gamer freak than a cool kid, sitting around with girls.

So I took my Game Boy out, sat on the bench and started playing it before I heard the bell. I turned my Game Boy off and hid it in my bag.

I went inside for my last lesson, which was P.E. according to my timetable.

Mr Mikeson was our P.E. teacher. He said, "Good afternoon, class! Today, we are going to do some running on the track – so boys, get changed, please, and meet me outside."

I took my P.E. bag and went into the boys' changing room. It really stank in there, so I covered my nose and mouth so I wouldn't throw up.

I changed really quickly, and then I went outside to meet Mr Mikeson while the others started showing up. A lot of them were taller and older than me – they could have been Caleb's age, fifteen or sixteen.

But I was the smallest out of all them, and I was a fast runner, so I beat a lot of them on the track, which made them jealous of me.

At last, they all came to meet me and Mr Mikeson. I was getting myself ready when Mr Mikeson blew his whistle. I was off. I ran and ran, until most of the boys couldn't keep up.

When the track race was over, I went to the toilet before going home. I didn't change out of my P.E. clothes, because I couldn't be bothered. Then I tied my blazer around my waist, got my shoulder bag on, and saw Daniel waiting at the gate for me.

I walked over to him. I almost held his hand, and then he said, "Tommy, I don't want you to hold my hand any more."

I said, "Ooh, okay then, birthday boy." I kept my hands to myself as we walked.

We got to the bus stop, and I sat down on the bench, putting my blazer in my bag.

Finally, the bus came, the doors opened and Daniel and I got on. I swiped my bus pass and said, "24 Ally Street – that's where we are getting off."

Daniel sat down on the back seat. I sat next to him and said, "Are you okay, birthday boy?"

Daniel said, "Yes, I am okay. Everyone wished me happy birthday at school today."

I smiled at him. "I am glad you're okay, and that's nice that everyone said happy birthday to you."

The bus stopped at Ally Street, the doors opened and we both got off and started walking home.

We got to the gate of our house and Daniel opened it. I went up to the doorstep, took my house key and opened the door. We went inside and I saw Harriet preparing food for Daniel's birthday party in the kitchen.

Harriet said, "Birthday boy! How was school today?"

Daniel said, "School was okay, and everyone said happy birthday to me."

Harriet said, "Aw! That's really sweet, Daniel. I can't believe you are eight. I remember you as that small seven-year-old boy."

Daniel's face turned red. "Yeah, I remember that too."

"The food smells nice," I said. "I can't wait to eat."

Daniel went upstairs to his room to get changed for his birthday party.

People started showing up at the house – Sarah and Caleb came, and also Daniel's school friends. Dad came in with his cake and put it on the table. I told everyone to hide, and then I quickly turned off the lights.

Daniel came downstairs and looked around. "Hello? Where is everyone?"

When he turned on the lights, we all jumped up and shouted, "SURPRISE! HAPPY BIRTHDAY, DANIEL!"

Daniel was shocked and said, "Wow, thanks, everyone."

I hugged him and laughed. "Happy birthday, buddy. I hope you enjoy it."

Dad came over with Daniel's birthday cake. He put the number eight candle on the cake, and we all sang happy birthday to him again.

After that, Dad flicked the lighter and gently touched it to the candle.

I said, "Make a wish, Daniel."

Daniel closed his eyes, made a wish and blew out the candle. He held the knife as Harriet got the camera and took some pictures of him. Daniel cut the cake and we all started eating and laughing together.

Daniel played and talked with a few of his friends from his class, while Sarah, Caleb and I started talking about teenage stuff Daniel and his friends don't know about.

Then the party was over and everyone started getting ready to go home, but Sarah and Caleb remained with us until their parents came to pick them up.

After they all left, Sarah and Caleb said, "We're going home now. Happy birthday, Daniel."

Daniel said, "Thank you both for coming. Bye."

I waved bye to them, and they waved bye back at me and Daniel.

I closed the door and lay on the sofa with Daniel, feeling tired.

Daniel yawned and said, "I had a good birthday. I have lots of cards and presents."

I also yawned. "I think we both should get ready for bed."

Daniel and I went upstairs, and then I went to my room and Daniel to his. I changed into my pyjamas, and then I put my lamp on and got into bed.

I started thinking about when I was eight. Many things had changed: Daniel and I no longer shared a room, and I behaved more like a big brother to Daniel, doing his hair and dressing him up. He tells me everything he wants now.

I liked our new house now. We'd cleaned it up, so it appeared nice and modern, but I also missed my mom at times, because she had always been there for me – unlike Harriet, who was there for Daniel more than me.

Dad had settled down, and he didn't drink like he did before. He and Harriet sort of got along with each other. He had been working at his new job, which was the reason we moved here.

Harriet and I still argued quite a lot, and it felt like she got along with Daniel more, but I tried to not argue with her and for us to get along. I tried to make her realise I was her son now, and she needed to allow me to be a thirteen-year-old boy. I am not two years old any more – that was when she last saw me, but that's in the past now.

I felt so sleepy – I couldn't keep my eyes open, so I fell asleep and had a dream that I was eight years old again. I dreamt I went back to our old house and it looked the same as always – the awkward square windows. I opened the door and went up to the cramped corner Daniel and I use to play in. The room looked brighter, but there was fog everywhere.

Then I heard, "What are you doing here Tommy?"

I turned around – it sounded like my mother. I said, "I left something here, so I am coming to collect it."

My mother said, "All right, Tommy." But then the voice changed, and I felt confused and clueless.

***

I opened one eye. My stepmother was by my bed. She asked me, "Tom, did you have a dream? I came here to wake you up for school, but you wouldn't wake up."

I said, "Oh, yes, I did have a dream, but it's none of your business."

I got up and went to the bathroom to brush my teeth and have a shower. When I was done, I went to my room to get dressed into my school clothes.

When I was done dressing up, I went downstairs to have breakfast. Daniel was already at the kitchen table eating. I sat down by him and started eating my Coco Pops. After that, I put my bowl and Daniel's in the sink, and I got my shoulder bag and coat on. Then I helped Daniel with his coat, bag and lunch box.

I got up and opened the door. I said bye to Harriet and then stood at the doorstep for Daniel to meet me. Eventually, he did. We walked to the bus stop and Daniel sat on the bench, while I remained standing and looking down at my watch, waiting for the bus to come.

The bus came a bit earlier than I expected. The doors opened and Daniel and I waited for the other people to get out. Then we both went inside and I swiped my bus pass. I said to the driver, "Northern Hills Middle School is I am getting off."

The driver said, "Thank you," and then I took my seat next to Daniel.

When the bus approached my school, I pressed the stop button and said, "Daniel, I'll see you at the gate after school."

Daniel said, "Okay – bye, Tommy. Have a good day."

I got off the bus and started walking to the school gate. It was open today, and I quickly got out my timetable to check what my first lesson was. Then I saw it in a bright red shaded box – it was music.

I looked at my watch and thought, *Oh, man, I am late already – Miss Jackson will give me detention now.* I ran down the corridor to TR45 – the music room.

I got to the door and Miss Jackson said, "Please wait outside, Tommy, until I am done."

I closed the door and waited for her to finish talking with the class.

Chapter Thirty-One

Then Miss Jackson came out and said, "Tommy, why are you late? You know the class starts at ten, and you got here at twelve. There are no excuses as to why you are late, because you tell me many excuses."

I groaned. "I had to help my little brother get ready for school, because my stepmother is too busy in the morning to do that, so I do everything for him."

Miss Jackson said, "Okay, Tommy, I'll let you off today, but the next time you are late there'll be a meeting with your parents, or detention with me."

"Yes, Miss. I'll try and come earlier."

I went inside, took off my jacket, put my bag on the floor and sat down. I got out my pen and notebook to jot down some notes.

I raised my hand and said, "Miss, can I go to the toilet, please?"

Miss Jackson said, "Are you desperate? If you are then you can go, but two minutes, Tommy."

"Yes, I am. Thank you, Miss."

I ran down to the boys' toilets, pushed the door open and went inside. Then I unfastened my belt, pulled down my boxers and started peeing. After I was done, I pulled up my boxers and fastened my belt. Then I went back to class and sat down.

Miss Jackson said, "Class is dismissed now. Everyone go for lunch."

The class started leaving and I was about to join the others.

Chapter Thirty-Two

Then Miss Jackson said, "Come here, please, Tommy. I need a word with you."

I went over to her desk and said, "Yes, Miss, I am here."

Miss Jackson said, "It's nothing bad – you're not in trouble or anything, but I am a bit cornered that you needed the toilet quite early. I don't know if your stepmother gave me that information for your file when you joined this school, so I am giving you a little note, and you can return it to me next week."

I said, "Yes, I will give her the note. Thank you so much."

"No problem, Tommy, sweetie – have a nice lunch."

I went outside to the playground and played on my Game Boy. I never eat at school because I end up sick. I remember eating fish and chips from the canteen and I threw up really badly. Since then, I've never eaten at school again. I always wait until I go home and eat.

After I was done playing my Game Boy, I hung my jacket over my shoulder bag and went inside for my last lesson. I looked down on my timetable. It was a light blue shaded box: English with Miss Anderson, and after that I could go home.

I went to the room where English was held, but Miss Anderson wasn't there. We had a different teacher – he was very nice, and we all introduced ourselves to him.

After that it was time to go home, so everyone ran out of the door, leaving me walking behind them.

Chapter Thirty-Three

Daniel was outside waiting for me at the gate, so I went over to him. I took his bag and we started walking home.

We got to the bus stop, and I sat down on the bench while Daniel stood beside me under the shelter. I looked at the bus timetable and it said the 178 bus should come now.

The bus was late but finally came. The doors opened and Daniel and I did our same routine, and then we both sat down.

The bus approached our street and I pressed the stop button. The doors opened and we both got off the bus, and then we started walking to the house gate.

The gate was already open. We went through it, and then Daniel and I stood by the doorstep, because I forgot to take my key that morning, so Harriet has to let us in.

She said, "Tom, why didn't you take your key this morning? I was busy in the garden – you know better than that."

I mumbled and groaned. "I was late for school. Miss Jackson nearly gave me a detention, and she told me to give you this note about my personal issues."

Harriet took the note and said, "Okay, I'll read it later, but you should have remembered before running late. I am pretty busy in the garden sorting out our shed – some stuff has broken in it."

I rolled my eyes before looking at the floor. "Why you are always blaming things on me, Harriet? You always say you're in the garden when you could just come in and help me!"

Harriet said, "Don't argue with me, young man! I am not ready to hear all that – go to your room!"

Chapter Thirty-Four

I threw my bag in front of her and went upstairs to my room. I slammed the door and sat down on my bed. I hated my stepmother so much. She always blamed me for everything and she didn't even look after me. We always had arguments because she always thought she was right, just like Brianna at school.

Sometimes I wished my mother was alive, because she didn't blame me for everything and we never argued all the time. Unlike Harriet – she was not like my mom at all. She was just my worst nightmare, someone who gave me problems all the time, and I didn't like being her stepson.

I was really angry, so I got under the covers and fell asleep.

***

Later, I woke up to a light in my room. A voice said, "Tommy, Harriet told me you were rude to her."

I noticed it was my dad, and I got up and said, "Because she was blaming me for leaving my house key at home this morning!"

Dad said, "There's no need to yell at me, mister! You and Harriet can't always argue when I am not here. I know sometimes you wish your mother was here, but we have to try and get along in this house. We are meant to be a family, Tom."

I said, "Is this what you are trying to tell me? Dad, you even dated her and I didn't know about it – ugh, I don't want to hear anymore!"

I ran out of my room, went downstairs and opened the door. I sat down outside on the door step and cried.

Dad came outside and kneeled down next to me.

Chapter Thirty-Five

I said, "Leave me alone! Dad, I'm not in the mood."

Dad said, "Tom, listen. I know you didn't like what I said, which made you upset enough to sit out here, but you need to try and give Harriet a chance, and things will be fine."

I said, "Okay, Dad. I will try and give her a chance."

Dad said, "Tom, dinner will be ready soon," and he went back inside.

"Okay, I'll be inside in a minute."

I went inside, wiped my feet on the door mat, and sat down next to Daniel. I had my dinner – it was pasta bake with potato chips.

After I was done eating, I took my plate and put it in the sink.

Harriet said, "Can your father and I have a word with you, Tom?"

I said, "Yes, okay – I'll wait in the living room." I knew they were going to talk about how I behaved towards Harriet after school that day.

Daniel went to his room to play, and Dad and my stepmother came and sat down.

Harriet said, "I can't find any of your documents about you, since we haven't really unpacked the letters about your personal issues."

Dad said, "I agree with Harriet, but tell Miss Jackson to give us a few days to look for them."

Chapter Thirty-Six

I said, "Okay then. I'll tell her that when I next see her."

I went upstairs to my room and lay down on my bed, watching the blank ceiling. I started to feel sleepy. The light came into my room. I knew it was Daniel, and I asked him, "Do you need something, Danny?"

Daniel said, "Can we play outside? There's nothing for me to do when you go to sleep."

I looked at him and said, "Okay, let me get dressed – I am a little bit tired, Daniel, but playing might wake me up."

Daniel came into my room and sat down on my beanbag. Then he looked away, because he knows I don't like being seen while I get changed.

When I was done, Daniel uncovered his eyes and said, "You're ready to go now, Tommy?"

I said, "Yes, I am – let's go downstairs and put our coats on, and then we are all set and ready to go."

We both went downstairs and got our jackets on. Harriet and Dad were fast asleep.

I opened the door and we both went outside. I took the ball and we played football together, and then I kicked the ball really high. Daniel ran over to catch the ball and brought it back.

I laughed at him. "You should have run faster than that, Daniel."

Daniel laughed back. "I tried running as fast as I could, Tommy."

It started to rain and I took the ball. Daniel started going back to the house, while I followed behind him.

The door was open, and we both went inside. Harriet and Dad had woken up while we were outside, and they both started cleaning the house.

I took off my jacket, helping Daniel take off his, and then I put the ball back in the corner where it belongs.

I took off my shoes and stayed in my socks after that. I helped Daniel with his shoes, which felt like a tug of war, because his shoes were very hard to take off.

I finally got his shoe off, which made me fall on the floor, and then I got to my feet. "Daniel, you wore these tug of war shoes for football – oh my gosh."

Daniel started laughing and said, "I didn't want to get my Converse dirty, so I had to wear the tug of war shoes, Tommy."

Dad suggested when the rain stops, we should go for a family meal.

Daniel said, "Yay, that sounds good – I love that we're all going out for a meal."

I said, "Me too – I haven't been to a meal for a long time now."

The rain finally stopped, and I went upstairs to take a shower. After that, I went to my room to get changed into my formal clothes.

I wore my suit and tie and brushed my hair, and also put a bit of perfume on.

Then Daniel went to the bathroom to have a shower. After he was done, Daniel went to his room to get changed to his suit. When he was done, I went to his room, helped him brush his hair and did his tie, and then we both went downstairs.

Harriet said, "You look smart and handsome."

Daniel said, "Thank you, Harriet."

I said, "Are we ready to go now, Harriet?"

Dad came over and said, "Yes, we are ready to go now."

I opened the door and we all went to the car, put our seat belts on, and Dad drove us to the restaurant. He parked in the car park and then we all got out and went inside.

Daniel and I picked what we were going to eat – it was going to be rice with some chicken and vegetables in it.

Harriet and Dad chose a British meal, with garlic bread and fish with lemon.

We all sat down at one table, and the waitress came with our orders. She also brought our drinks which she might have forgotten about. We all started enjoying the food, munching away.

After that it was getting late, so we got our coats on and started heading to the car. We all got our seat belts on and drove to the house. Dad parked up on our driveway and I opened my door – I let Daniel scoot over to use mine and we both got out.

I took my key, opened the door and we all went inside. I put on the lights because it was really dark out.

Daniel and I took off our coats and went to the living room to watch TV. Dad and Harriet took off their coats and came to sit down with us.

Then Daniel went upstairs to get ready for bed, and I continued watching TV until I felt sleepy, and I went upstairs to my room.

When I got there, I took off my suit and tie and changed into my pyjamas. I got under the covers and put on my lamp, and then I fell asleep for the night.

***

The following morning, the window started making slapping noises, like it was opening and closing. I woke up feeling clueless, and the coldness in the room made my body shake. Everything was flying around violently as the wind blew.

I tried to stand up, but the wind pushed me down to the floor. I felt the side of my stomach begin to stab me – I was in pain, but I didn't know what was going on or what I was doing. I felt I was dreaming, but I wasn't.

I went to the bathroom and started brushing my teeth, and then I started to throw up. I saw blood on the sink, and I looked blank at the mirror. Then I realised something was wrong with me, because I had never seen blood after throwing up in my entire life.

I didn't even continue brushing my teeth. I went downstairs and said, "Harriet, I don't feel all right. I threw up blood, which I've never done before."

Harriet said, "What do you want me to do about it, Tom? Go to your father – I am busy."

My stepmother changed after I spoke to her. I thought to myself, *She might be evil and not want me to live, because I don't exist to her.*

I went to my dad and told him everything. He said, "Maybe you have an infection."

I said, "Okay, Dad – maybe I do."

I went upstairs to my room, got into bed and went back to sleep.

***

I woke up and Dad said, "Put your clothes on – we are going to the doctors, Tom."

I got up, put my clothes on and went downstairs. Dad and I started walking to the bus stop. When I got on the bus, I saw Sarah sitting in the back seat.

Sarah asked me, "Where are you going, Tom?"

I said, "I don't feel very well, so I'm going to the doctors."

Sarah gave me a sad look. "I hope you feel better. I don't like it when you are sick."

"I'll be okay. Where are you going, Sarah?"

"I am going to see an old friend I haven't seen in ages."

I wanted to stay longer with her, and then Dad said, "We are here now, Tom."

I said to her, "I am going now. I'll see you later, Sarah."

Sarah said, "Okay, see you later, Tom. I hope you feel better."

I got off the bus and we started walking to the hospital.

Dad asked me, "Hmm, this Sarah girl you were talking to in the back – is she your girlfriend?"

I felt my face going red. "No! Dad, she's not my girlfriend! She's just a good friend to me and everything."

Dad started laughing. "Okay, I was only asking, Tom."

We both started laughing together. When we got to the hospital we had settled down.

I sat down on the waiting chairs, and Dad went to the front desk to book the appointment for me. Then Dad came and sat down with me, and I started playing the Game Boy.

The doctor shouted, "Tommy Dawson, here!"

I got up and took my Game Boy and jacket. Dad followed behind me. We went to room sixteen and sat down.

The doctor said, "I am Doctor James. Introduce yourself to me, please, young man."

I said, "I am Tommy Dawson, and I was feeling really sick this morning. I felt dizzy and went to the bathroom to brush my teeth, and I threw up blood in the sink."

Doctor James said, "Let me look at your throat, Tommy, and see if there's an infection."

I opened my mouth, and Doctor James used a light to look at my throat.

Doctor James said, "Your throat is a little bit red and sore, but it's nothing serious. The dizziness might have been too much thinking. Are you having a difficult time in your life, Tom? Did you lose someone in your family?"

I felt a pool of tears come to my eyes, and they soon started rolling down my cheeks. I wiped my eyes and said, "My mom passed away when I was eight years old due to a car accident, and ever since then I never felt happy. I live with my stepmother."

Dad said, "It makes him think quite a lot. He doesn't get on with his stepmother at all."

Doctor James said, "Why you don't get on with your stepmother, Tom?"

I wiped my tears. "Because she doesn't love me, and she treats me like a child in front of people."

Dad looked surprised. "So you weren't happy about moving here to live with her? Why didn't you tell me in the first place, Tom?"

"Dad! Because you were happy about your new job, and I didn't want to ruin it for you."

Doctor James said, "You should get a counsellor and share what you are going through with them. They will give you some advice."

I said, "Where would I find one to share some things with?"

Doctor James said, "I'll give you one, Tom, and maybe she will be a female so she will understand you."

Dad said, "Thank you, Doctor James – this would help us understand what's been going on with Tom."

Doctor James said, "You are very welcome, Mr Dawson."

I said, "Thank you, Doctor James – you are very nice."

Doctor James said, "You are most welcome, Tommy, and thank you."

Dad and I got up, left Doctor James' office and started making our way home.

We got to the bus stop. The bus arrived and I found a seat.

When we approached our house, I pressed the stop button. The bus went to the bus stop, the doors opened and Dad and I got off.

We got to our gate. I stood beside Dad as he opened the door and we both went inside.

Daniel was already home from school, and he was in the living room watching TV.

I asked him, "When I was in hospital, were you in my room?"

He looked down at the floor and said, "Yes, to read the book you don't want me to see."

I looked at him in anger. "I told you not to read it, didn't I?"

Daniel said, "You did! I wanted to know why, but now I do know why – because you miss your mom in those pictures!"

I said, "That is not it – there are some things in that book you're too young to know about. I can't believe you, Daniel!"

Daniel looked at me in tears. "I'm sorry, all right? I didn't mean to read it."

My heart sank and I felt like crying as well, but I stayed strong and held it in. "I'm sorry I was mad at you, and I should have told you from the beginning what the real reason not to read it was."

Daniel said, "It's okay – I shouldn't have gone to your room without asking you first, and I am sorry, Tommy."

He came over and gave me a hug, which made me cry. The hug was warm and comfortable, and it gave me a flashback of my mom hugging me when I was eight years old. If I was hurt or sad, my mom gave me the same hug Daniel gave me now.

Daniel asked, "Tommy, were you crying?"

I cleared my throat, made my face look normal, and wiped my nose so he wouldn't notice I was crying. "No, I wasn't – something was in my eye"

I went upstairs to my room, and I went on my laptop. I had a message saying: *Sarah Wright added you on Web chat.*

I thought, *Sarah must have accepted my friend request.*

I typed: *Hi, Sarah. It's Tommy.*

Then it said: *Sarah Wright is writing,* and then the message appeared: *Oh, hello, Tom – are you okay now?*

I replied: *I am a bit better – the doctor said the dizziness came from too much thinking, and I might need some advice about some personal things.*

Again, I saw the words: *Sarah Wright is typing,* and then it disappeared and appeared again.

Sarah said: *Yes, you might need some advice, and I'm sure it would help you. I might come to your house and check if you're okay, maybe on Friday.*

I said: *It would be great for you to come home – even Daniel asks of you a lot.*

Sarah said: *I'll be back in one minute Tommy – I'm going to help Caleb out with something.*

I said: *Okay, I'll wait for you to come back.*

Her chat profile changed to the busy red sign, and then it turned back to green.

Sarah said: *I am back now, Tommy – did I take long?*

I said through the webcam, "No, you didn't – I went to the bathroom, and Daniel wanted me for something."

Also on webcam, Sarah said, "Oh, okay – I'm glad you're back. Tell Daniel I said hello."

I said, "Okay, I'll tell him, and tell Caleb I said hi, and also your dad."

When the conversation was over, I went downstairs for dinner. I sat down at the kitchen table.

Harriet said, "You are late for dinner, Tom."

"Oh, I was doing some homework in my room," I lied. "That's why I was late."

Harriet looked at me. "All right then, Tom. Make sure you do your homework earlier next time."

I said, "Okay, I will. I need to go back and continue on it."

I went upstairs to my room, closed my door, and went back on my laptop to sign into web chat. Sarah appeared online.

Hi, Sarah – it's me again. I had something to say.

Sarah typed back: Hi, Tom. Did you want to remind me about something before leaving?

I replied: *I'll tell you on Friday – I have forgotten now.*

Sarah said: *All right then, Tom. I'll see you on Friday.*

I received a message to say the web chat ended. I closed my laptop, and got under the covers. I turned my lamp on, and then I fell asleep.

I started thinking about Sarah and how helpful she had been to me. I thought, *I mean, no one would have been there like she has been. I hope counsellor will be nice to me.*

Friday morning came. I woke up and went to the bathroom to brush my teeth and have a shower. After that, I went to my room to put on my school uniform. I also brushed my hair and put my shoes on.

I went downstairs to have breakfast. Daniel was already eating. I sat on my chair beside him, and I started eating my breakfast too. When I was done eating, I put our bowls in the sink.

I got my shoulder bag and put my coat on, and then I helped Daniel put on his coat and backpack.

Dad came and said, "Bye, boys – have a school day at school."

Daniel and I said, "Bye, Dad – we'll see you later."

I opened the door, and we started making our way to the bus stop. It was raining, so we put our hoods up so we wouldn't get wet.

By the time we had reached the bus stop shelter, it had stopped raining a little. Daniel sat on the bench, looking at the puddle on the floor.

Chapter Thirty-Seven

I remained standing the whole time, looking down at my watch, waiting for the 178 bus to come.

I thought to myself, *I hope it won't be the 179 bus, because it's always full of people.*

The 178 bus came and the doors opened. Daniel and I went inside.

I swiped my bus pass and said, "Northern Hills Middle School, please."

Daniel went to pick a seat at the back, and he sat down and waited for me. I sat down by him.

When we reached my school I pressed the stop button. "Daniel, have a good day at school, and remember to meet me at the gate like always."

Daniel said, "Okay, Tommy, I will do that, and you too."

I got off the bus and started heading to the school entrance.

When I got there, and I looked down at my timetable. There was a box shaded in light green – it said art was my first lesson.

I went down the corridor. The art room was CB56, and Miss Alison opened the door and let me in.

I sat down and asked her, "Where is everyone?"

Miss Alison said, "Tom, you are a bit early and the lesson hasn't started yet."

I said, "Oh, I might doodle on my notebook then."

I got out my notebook, which was spotty and had stripes in different colours.

The class started showing up, and that time I was done doodling in my notebook.

After art class, I went outside and sat on the same bench, playing my Game Boy.

After the break was over I went back inside, and I looked at my timetable. It was shaded light blue and said "history". I went down the hall and went to SHG89 that was the history class room.

I went to the room and Mr Henderson said, "Class, come in and sit down, please, so we can get the lesson started."

I went in and sat down, and then I waited for everyone else to come in too.

The class finally came in, which took forever and I was waiting for ages.

Anyway, everyone settled down and the lesson began. We learned about what life was like in the olden days, and how difficult education was, and how people lived in those times.

When the class was over, everyone got ready to go home, and Daniel was already waiting at the gate for me.

I went over to him, and then I saw a girl beside him, waving. I noticed Daniel and Sarah must have come together to meet me.

Sarah giggled and said, "Hi, Tom. I became a student at your school this afternoon with Daniel."

I laughed at the joke, and I said, "Yes, you did, Sarah. So Daniel didn't give you any trouble?"

Daniel looked shocked and said, "Tommy! How dare you say that? I never give anyone trouble, unlike you."

Sarah laughed. "Don't listen to your brother. He's only messing around with you, Daniel."

We all started making our way to the bus stop together.

Sarah asked me, "Tom, do you think your advice person would help you with the relationship between you and Harriet?"

I shrugged at her. "I don't know, Sarah – we have to wait and see. Maybe I'll meet her this week, or she might come to school."

Sarah said, "Oh, right – that would be cool. I'm sure she will be lovely."

We made it to the bus stop, and Daniel sat down on the bench, while Sarah and I continued talking.

The bus came and the doors opened. Daniel sat in the front seat, and Sarah and I sat at the back.

Sarah and I remained talking, and I pressed the stop button, so the driver knows we would be getting off soon.

The bus stopped, the doors opened, and the three of us got off and started making our way back to the house.

We got the gate and I got out my house key. Sarah and Daniel came behind me. I opened the door and we all went inside.

Harriet said, "Hello, boys. So how was school today? And hi, Sarah – are you all right?"

Sarah said, "Hi, Mrs Robinson. Yes, I am fine, thanks – you? We are going to do some homework together, Tom and I."

I said, "School was okay. Sarah is here to help me with the math homework."

Harriet said, "Okay then, you two – if you need anything, I'll be in the living room."

Sarah and I said, "That's fine, Harriet – tell us when dinner is ready."

Sarah and I went upstairs to my room. I put on the lights, and Sarah sat down on my beanbag in the corner of my room.

I closed the door and said, "We need to think of a plan of how I'll speak to the counsellor."

Sarah said, "I think if the counsellor is nice then you will have more chance of speaking honestly to her."

I thought quietly about what Sarah said for a moment, and then I agreed that maybe she was right, but it depended on the person.

I said, "You are right, Sarah. I was just thinking how I agree."

Sarah laughed and said, "I told you, silly. I know you'll be fine with the counsellor – just don't panic, Tom." She ate a piece of chocolate chip cookie from the packet and said, "Do you want help with the science homework?"

I said, "Yes, please – on page 134, about the stomach."

Sarah took the science book and turned over to page 134.

I said "Wow, that's pretty interesting, but what does this mean?"

"Hmm, it's reflecting how small our stomachs are, Tom."

"Oh, really? That's amazing, isn't it, Sarah?"

Sarah said, "Tom, I think I have to go home now. It's getting late and I promised my dad I'd be home by six. I will speak to you on web chat."

Chapter Thirty-Eight

I said, "Oh, okay, Sarah. Take care – I'll see you on web chat. My laptop will be by me."

Sarah left my room and went downstairs. I heard her telling Harriet she was going, and then she went home.

I got on my laptop and signed in to web chat. Soon Sarah's chat profile turned green, which meant she was online.

I did a video call to see if she was there, and then she appeared.

Sarah said, "Hello, Tom. I am home now."

I replied, "Hi, Sarah. That's good that you are home now."

"Did you copy the notes I wrote down for you about the stomach?"

"Yes, I did write it down – one second, let me get it."

"Take your time. I will be waiting, Tom".

I went over to my desk, came back and showed her the paper. "That's all the information I wrote down about the stomach," I said.

Sarah replied, "Your science teacher will be happy about that."

After the chat, I went downstairs for dinner. I didn't want Harriet to say I was late again.

However, when I got downstairs dinner wasn't ready yet, so I sat down and waited with Daniel.

Harriet put our dinners on the plates. It was macaroni and cheese with a bit of salad on the side.

I started eating, and I spat out my food on the plate because it was really hot.

Harriet said, "You should have been patient before eating, Tom."

I said, "I know that, Harriet. You didn't need to tell me."

Harriet went quiet and was surprised, but she couldn't think of anything to say.

I continued eating. After I was done, I went to my room and started writing up the facts about the stomach on my laptop.

When I was finished, I got into bed, and I remembered that after the weekend it would be Monday, and I would meet the counsellor at school for the first time.

Monday morning came, and I got out of bed and did my daily routine.

I got my shoes on and went downstairs. Daniel was already dressed and ready.

I sat down and had breakfast at the table with Daniel before getting my coat and shoulder bag on. I helped Daniel with his coat and bag and I carried his lunchbox for him.

Daniel said bye to Dad and Harriet, and then I closed the door. We were off to the bus stop now.

Daniel and I got to the bus stop, and I remained standing up, waiting for the bus to come. As usual, Daniel remained sitting down on the bench.

The bus finally came and the doors opened. I swiped my bus pass, and I told the driver, "Northern Hills Middle School, please."

Daniel picked the front seat, and I sat down with him, giving him his lunchbox.

Soon I pressed the stop button, and I said, "Daniel, have a good day, and remember to wait for me at the gate."

Daniel said, "Of course I will. See you later."

I got off the bus and started walking to the school gate. When I got there, I looked at my time table and saw a light blue shaded box. It said English was my first lesson.

I went to the room and Miss Anderson said, "Tom, your counsellor might be coming to visit you today – I think her name is Lindsey."

I said, "Oh, okay. Thank you, Miss Anderson."

I took a seat and listened to what Miss Anderson was teaching us.

After a while someone appeared at the door. The person said, "Um, hello. I am looking for Tommy Dawson."

Miss Anderson said, "Tom, she is here now. I'll see you later then."

I said, "Okay, Miss Anderson."

I went out of the room with the counsellor and into one of the empty classrooms. We sat down together.

"Let me introduce myself," she said. "My Name is Lindsey Miller, and I am the counsellor who helps young people your age in the difficult times they go through in their lives. I heard from your doctor you have a rough time with your stepmother. Well, tell me about yourself and we'll talk about that."

I said, "I am Tommy Dawson and I am thirteen years old. My mother died when I was eight years old, and my father got a new job when I was twelve. I had to live with my stepmother Harriet Robinson, and we basically fight a lot about most things. She treats me like a two-year-old around my brother Daniel and my friends, and sometimes I feel like she abuses me."

Lindsey grabbed her notebook and said, "I am going to write this down. So after you went through this, did you feel like doing anything to yourself?"

I said, "I did go through a mild depression when I was missing my mom. I didn't self-harm or anything – I just felt sad a lot."

Lindsey said, "All right, so how old is your brother now, and how does he feel about everything?"

"He's just turned eight, and he seems happy with everything, but I never got to ask him how he feels about them right now."

"Okay then, Tommy, so what is his name, and how old was he when your mother died?"

I said, "His name is Daniel, and he was about three that time."

Lindsey laughed and said, "I am jotting down everything you said, so I might have to discuss this with your parents."

I felt a pool of tears come to my eyes as I looked down at the floor.

Lindsey said, "Aw! Are you all right, Tommy? I'm sorry."

She left her notebook and pen on the chair, and came over to give me a hug.

I hugged her and nodded. "I'm sorry. I just felt emotional about the whole thing."

Chapter Thirty-Nine

Lindsey said, "You don't have to be sorry. I know how it feels to lose someone you love, but you were so strong and brave to talk about this. I mean, I've worked with many boys your age, and they couldn't even tell me one word. They just end up crying."

I smiled. "Thank you, Lindsey. You are very nice."

Lindsey laughed and said, "It's my pleasure, Tommy." She grabbed her notebook, jacket and bag. "I have to go now, Tommy, but I hope I'll meet you again at home." She gave me a hug and left the empty class room.

I said, "Okay, I'll be looking forward to it. Bye, Lindsey."

Then I went back to the classroom. The class was gone, which meant it was break time now. But Miss Anderson told me to come in. I went in and sat down.

I said, "Miss Anderson, everything went well, and Lindsey was nice."

Miss Anderson said, "That's what I wanted to hear, Tom. You can go for break now."

I got up, taking my bag and jacket, closed the door, and I went for break.

I went to the same picnic table, and sat down playing my Game Boy, since I didn't see Lester around.

After the break was over, I looked at my timetable. I had P.E. with Mr Mikeson again.

I went to the sports hall with my P.E. bag, and the other boys joined me. P.E. has always been separated, because there wasn't enough space to do it in the same hall as the girls.

Anyway, Mr Mikeson said, "Boys, we are going to do some stretching today, so get changed, please."

We all did as were told and went to the boys changing room.

It didn't stink like last time, so they must have sprayed the room. They hardly ever do, and most of the boys in my class don't even have a shower.

I changed really quickly into my shorts and t-shirt, put on my trainers, put my school uniform in my P.E. bag and closed it, and then I left the changing room.

I put my P.E. bag in the pile the boys put theirs. Mine had my name on it so it wouldn't get mixed up. Then I went over to join them, and I sat down on the floor like they all did.

Mr Mikeson said, "Boys, stand up, and let's start with stretching our arms and making circles with them."

We got up and did as he asked.

Mr Mikeson said, "Now, as you're jumping, bring your legs up and down."

We did this, and I fell on the floor really hard.

I winced in pain, and Mr Mikeson came over. He said, "Are you okay, Tom?"

I said, "No! I hurt my leg, and I can't get up!"

One of the boys, who looked about my age, said, "I'll help you up with my friend." He called the other boy over. They helped me up from the floor and walked with me slowly to the bench. The same other boy brought my P.E. bag to me.

I thanked them both, and they said no problem and that it was a pleasure. Then they both went back to doing the jumping activity.

Mr Mikeson came over to me and said, "You can't do P.E. with us, Tom, but you can watch."

I said, "Okay, I will watch you guys do it."

I watched them do the activity, which looked like fun, but I couldn't join in since I'd hurt my leg.

The lesson was over, and I got up slowly, limping to the gate to go home.

Daniel was at the gate, and he said, "Are you all right, Tommy?"

I winced. "No, I hurt my leg in P.E."

"Do you want me to run get Dad? You can't walk like this."

I said, "No, I'll manage it – the bus stop isn't far, Danny."

"Okay – if you say so, Tommy."

Daniel and I started making our way to the bus stop. I walked slowly because my leg was still painful, and my knee was swollen by now.

We finally made it to the bus stop, and I sat down on the bench because of my leg injury.

The bus came more quickly than I expected. I got up slowly, giving Daniel my bus pass to swipe for me. When he had done that, I went to sit in the front row of the bus.

Chapter Forty

I told Daniel to get up, and press the stop button.

Daniel got up and tried to reach the stop button, but he couldn't press it.

I heard someone's voice. It said, "I'll help you press it."

It was the boy who helped me up from P.E. that day. I smiled at him and he smiled back. He said, "Don't worry, your leg will get better."

I said, "Thank you for helping us."

The boy said, "My pleasure, Tom."

The bus stopped, and Daniel and I got off and started making our way home.

Daniel opened the gate, went through, and stood on the doorstep.

I came to the doorstep, got my house key, and opened the door.

Harriet said, "Boys, how was school today?"

Daniel said, "School was okay. We went on a trip to the zoo."

I said, "No, it wasn't okay for me. I hurt my leg in P.E. today, and my knee is swollen."

Harriet said, "Let me look at your knee, Tom."

I raised my left leg a little bit for her to see the injury. My knee skin was red and swollen.

Harriet said, "I'll give you an icepack to cool the swelling down."

I said, "Okay then – I'll go and sit down."

Chapter Forty-One

I sat down on the sofa, putting my left leg on the coffee table.

Harriet came back with the icepack and said, "Put this on your knee, Tom – you might feel pain because it's cold."

I put the icepack on my knee. I nearly screamed – it was so cold and icy.

I said, "I think I won't need the icepack any more, Harriet."

Daniel giggled. "Wow, that must have given you brain freeze, Tom."

I stared at Daniel with a grin on my face. "It didn't give me brain freeze."

Harriet said, "Leave the icepack on the table, and then I'll come and collect it."

I left it on the table, and stared at the news on the TV.

After flicking through boring channels for a while, I decided to limp up to my room and speak with Sarah.

I got to my room, put my laptop on, and got on web chat.

Sarah wasn't online, so I surfed around on the internet looking at weird things that made me laugh a little bit, before getting comfortable on my bed and falling asleep.

I woke up to a knock on the front door, and I went downstairs to open it. I knew the counsellor was coming today.

Lindsey said, "Hello Tom. It's me, the counsellor you spoke with at school."

I said, "Oh, hello, Lindsey. Come in, and make yourself at home."

Lindsey came in and said to the others, "Hello, I am Lindsey Miller, Tommy's counsellor."

Dad said, "Nice to meet you, Lindsey. I am Adrian, Tommy's dad."

Lindsey took a seat and got herself settled in.

Daniel looked surprised, and he said, "Hello, Lindsey."

Lindsey looked closely at him. "Oh, hello. You must be Daniel, Tommy's little brother, right?"

Daniel nodded. "Yes, I am his brother."

Harriet came over and said, "Hello, I am Harriet, Tommy's stepmother, and you are?"

Lindsey said, "Hello, Harriet. I am Lindsey, Tommy's counsellor. I work with boys around Tommy's age who faces family problems and difficulties in their life."

Chapter Forty-Two

Lindsey said, "I am here to talk to Harriet, the stepmother, and Adrian, Tommy's dad. Basically, it's nothing bad – just about what Tommy feels about the whole problem."

Daniel said, "I am going to my room."

I saw him bundle up the stairs to his room, closing the door.

Lindsey said, "Tommy has told me about how he has been treated by you, Harriet. I would like you to tell me why you treat him like this."

Harriet said, "Tom never listens to me, and I find it hard to control him sometimes because I am not Susan, his real mother, so I see Tommy a bit differently."

Lindsey said, "Okay, I would like to give you advice at the end of our session. I think if you talk with Tommy nicely you might avoid fights."

Harriet said, "I try to, but he wouldn't accept it."

I said, "You're lying. I do listen to you, and you treat me like a two-year-old in front of everybody. You don't even care for me – what type of step mother are you?"

Lindsey said, "Calm down, Tommy, please – we need to sort this out."

Dad said, "Lindsey, do you think Tommy has any mental problems? We can't control him sometimes."

Lindsey said, "Probably anger issues and mild depression, Mr Dawson."

Dad said, "I see, Lindsey. He never shares anything with us."

Lindsey said, "Oh, I see. Maybe I'll have a word with Tom and see if he needs some help with these problems."

"Okay. Thank you so much, Lindsey."

"No problem, Mr Dawson. You both can go away now while I have a word with Tom."

Dad and Harriet went away, and it was just me and Lindsey. I looked down at the floor.

Lindsey said, "Tom, can you look at me, please?"

I raised my head and looked at her, playing with my fingers. I said, "I don't like my stepmother!"

Lindsey said, "I know, Tom, but let me speak or I can't help you."

I kept quiet and listened to her.

"You and Harriet don't get along – I can see that, but right now I need to find a plan to make you and Harriet understand each other."

"I don't want to live with her or get along with her. I want a different stepmother, because she doesn't even look after me, and we are always arguing!"

"All right, Tom – if that's what you want, I have to speak with your dad and see what he'll say."

I said, "All right then – thank you, Lindsey."

Lindsey wrote down: *Mr Dawson, Tom wants a new stepmother – we would like to know if you agree with this or not.*

She said, "I'll come back to you in a minute, Tom – I'm going to find your dad."

Lindsey went to the kitchen and closed the door. I heard her say, "Mr Dawson, can I have a word with you?"

Dad said, "Okay, Lindsey – what is it about?"

Chapter Forty-Three

Lindsey said, "I had a word with Tom, and he doesn't want Harriet as his stepmother anymore. If he wants a new stepmother, what do you think? I am going back to Tom to discuss it with him, with your agreement."

Dad said, "Lindsey, I even feel sorry for Tom, because I thought Harriet would be a good stepmother to him, but I have seen she is not. Harriet does treat him like a two-year-old, but because I like Harriet I ignored her. It's about time I show Tommy I am his father. Tom is thirteen now, and Daniel is eight – it is not suitable for him, seeing all these problems happening, so I agree with Tom for him to have a new stepmother."

Lindsey nodded and said, "I know what you're saying. You have agreed, so since I am his counsellor I will sort all this out for you."

"Thank you so much, Lindsey."

"You're welcome, Mr Dawson – it's my pleasure."

Lindsey unlocked the kitchen door and came back to me.

She said, "Okay, Tom – your dad and I were talking about the whole situation, and we both came to an agreement that you might need a new stepmother, because it is not fair on you and your brother."

I said, "Okay – I think that would solve many problems, if she goes and someone else takes her place."

Lindsey said, "I agree with you both. I will go away and write up this report for your school and also Doctor James." She added, "I am going now, Tom – I'll see you again probably."

I said, "Okay – bye, Lindsey, and thank you."

Lindsey left the house. I went upstairs to my room, and I fell asleep.

***

I woke up and went downstairs to have dinner.

It was the same macaroni and cheese left over from a few days ago, but I didn't really mind, so I took a chair, sat down and started eating.

After I was done eating, I went outside for a walk, and I sat down on the park bench. It was a bit cold and breezy in the park, but it was sunny outside.

All the trees looked brown, and the leaves had fallen off, leaving leaf marks on the ground.

It started to rain, and I ran back to the house.

When I got back to the house, I saw Harriet, and it seemed she had been taken away from the house.

I asked the officers what was going on. The police officer said, "I found your stepmother drinking, trying to kill your dad with a blade knife."

I said, "Oh, I see – so I'll be getting my new step mother soon?"

The officer said, "Basically, yes – your stepmother is violent, and your dad rang us to tell us to come."

So they took her in the police car and drove away.

Dad came and hugged me. "I'm sorry for everything I have done, Tom. I love you and I hope you know that."

I hugged my dad and Daniel too. I said, "Thank you for being there for me, and I am sorry too."

After everything cleared up, I had a new step mother. She was much more amazing than Harriet. Lindsey did come back to the house, and she asked how Emily was.

I said, "She's amazing and has really helped the family!"

The house was happy and cheerful – even Dad was happy about our new stepmother. Sometimes I did miss my mom, but I know she was smiling up there at me too.

Chapter Forty-Four

I went to her grave again. I said, "Hello, Mom. I know you miss me, and I miss you too. I have a new stepmother now. Her name is Emily, and she reminds me of you a lot, Mom."

I kissed her gravestone, leaving the park where she was buried. I went back to the house, and Emily asked me, "Sweetie, did you go and pay your mom your respects?"

I said, "Yes, Emily, I did. I hope she loves it."

Emily smiled. "Your mom really loved it – trust me."

We went inside before it rained, and we had dinner.

Dad went out for a while, and he came back home with a brown box.

When Daniel and I opened it, we found the most beautiful dog I had ever seen. It was black, and his nose shone in the light. His tail wagged happily. It was a boy.

Daniel said, "What are we going to name him?"

Emily looked at Dad. "What should we name him? He's part of the family now."

I said, "We should name him Jamie Jack Dawson."

Daniel said, "That's a cool name for him."

Emily laughed. "I love that name for him – it's adorable."

Dad said, "I agree with everyone. Welcome to the family, Jamie."

To this day, we spend a lot of time with Jamie. He is a very lovely dog.